THE BOBBSEY TWINS
CAMPING OUT

To Heather

FROM Billy

JuLY 6 th 1960

"I think we had better stay here for a while"

The Bobbsey Twins Camping Out

By

LAURA LEE HOPE

Published by

WORLD DISTRIBUTORS (MANCHESTER) LIMITED

LONDON – MANCHESTER

ENGLAND

THE BOBBSEY TWINS BOOKS

By Laura Lee Hope

THE BOBBSEY TWINS
THE BOBBSEY TWINS AT SCHOOL
THE BOBBSEY TWINS IN THE COUNTRY
THE BOBBSEY TWINS AT MEADOW BROOK
THE BOBBSEY TWINS AT THE SEASHORE
THE BOBBSEY TWINS ON A HOUSEBOAT
THE BOBBSEY TWINS CAMPING OUT
THE BOBBSEY TWINS ON BLUEBERRY ISLAND
THE BOBBSEY TWINS AT SNOW LODGE
THE BOBBSEY TWINS' WONDERFUL SECRET
THE BOBBSEY TWINS AT THE CIRCUS
THE BOBBSEY TWINS SOLVE A MYSTERY
THE BOBBSEY TWINS AT WHITESAIL HARBOUR
THE BOBBSEY TWINS AT MYSTERY MANSION
THE BOBBSEY TWINS IN RAINBOW VALLEY
THE BOBBSEY TWINS AND THE HORSESHOE RIDDLE
THE BOBBSEY TWINS AT BIG BEAR POND
THE BOBBSEY TWINS ON A BICYCLE TRIP
THE BOBBSEY TWINS TREASURE HUNTING
THE BOBBSEY TWINS AT SUGAR MAPLE HILL
THE BOBBSEY TWINS IN ESKIMO LAND
THE BOBBSEY TWINS AT LIGHTHOUSE POINT
THE BOBBSEY TWINS IN ECHO VALLEY
THE BOBBSEY TWINS ON THE PONY TRAIL

First impression 1955
Reprinted 1956
Reprinted 1957
Reprinted 1958

Printed in Great Britain by Jarrold & Sons Ltd, Norwich

CONTENTS

CHAPTER I

DINAH'S DUCKING

"FATHER has a secret!" Nan Bobbsey whispered this in the ear of her brother Bert who was idly swinging in the hammock stretched between two trees in the front garden.

"A secret!" exclaimed Bert, sitting up so suddenly that he nearly fell out of the hammock. "What do you mean—a secret?"

"Hush!" exclaimed Nan, motioning towards Flossie and Freddie, the younger twins, who were in another part of the garden digging a hole. "Don't let them hear you or they'll pester the life out of me to tell them what the secret is. And I don't know what it is myself," added Nan, with a laugh and a shake of her head that threw her brown curls in a tangled mass before her brown eyes.

"Then how do you know it's a secret?" asked Bert.

He moved to one end of the hammock to make room for Nan to sit beside him. Now whether Bert did it purposely or not I can't say, but no sooner had Nan sat in the hammock than both she and Bert fell with a thump out on the ground.

Luckily there was plenty of thick, green grass beneath the hammock. It had not been worn off, for the hammock had been in place only one day, and scuffling feet, used to swing it to and fro, had not yet destroyed the turf.

"Oh, look what you did!" cried Nan when she found herself on the grass.

"I did not! You did it yourself!" protested Bert. "Do you think I'd dump myself out, too?"

This sounded reasonable. Certainly, why should he spill himself, even if he did want to tip Nan out of the hammock on to the grass? As I said, I don't know whether Bert did it purposely or not.

Anyhow, he and Nan fell out of the hammock. The sound of their thumping fall and their cries brought Flossie and Freddie on the run from the place where the younger twins had been digging.

"Oh, look! Nan and Bert fell out of the hammock!" cried Flossie, shaking her golden curls.

"Do it again so we can see you!" begged Freddie, his blue eyes, just like those of Flossie, shining with eagerness.

"Do it again! I guess not much!" exclaimed Bert, as he scrambled to his feet and helped Nan to arise. "I gave my elbow a hard whack."

"And I think my knee is skinned," added Nan. "Don't say anything about the secret," she whispered in Bert's ear.

"How can I when I don't know it and you don't know it?" he inquired, more loudly.

"Hush!" whispered Nan, but it was too late. The sharp ears of Flossie and Freddie had caught the words.

"What is it?" cried Flossie. "What is it you want Bert to hush about, Nan?"

"Why can't you tell us?" Freddie wanted to know.

"Because there isn't anything to tell," said Nan, truthfully enough. She looked sharply at Bert. He did not seem very curious as he looked at the hammock ropes to make sure they were in proper place so there would be no more spills.

"Want to sit here and swing?" Bert asked of Nan, as once more he settled himself in the hammock.

"Thank you, no," she answered. "I don't want to be dumped out again."

"I didn't do it!" protested Bert, but Nan acted as if she didn't believe him.

"Well, if I hear anything I'll tell you later," she announced, as she walked away.

"What?" cried Flossie.

"What you going to tell him?" Freddie demanded.

"You twins run off and play what you were playing," advised Nan, with a laugh. "Were you digging down to China?" she asked, as she looked towards the hole Flossie and Freddie had been making.

"No, we're digging a well," explained Freddie, as he and his small twin sister moved slowly back to their play-spot. The golden-haired twins had plainly given up trying to find out what Nan and

Bert had been talking about when the hammock spill happened.

"We're digging a well," went on Flossie, "and Sam Johnson is squirting with the hose and we want him to squirt some water in our well-hole to make it real, but he won't."

"We could squirt water in the hole ourselves if he'd let us take the hose," said Freddie.

"But he won't!" exclaimed Flossie. "He won't let us do anything! He says we'll squirt on somebody and make a mess. But we wouldn't, would we, Freddie?"

"No!" answered Flossie's brother. "But Sam Johnson won't ever let us do nothin'! I don't care, come on, Flossie, we'll make a dry well."

"It'll be just as much fun," decided Flossie.

As the smaller twins walked slowly towards their "well", Bert got in the hammock again and swung to and fro. He watched Nan going back to the house, whence she had come to tell him that Mr. Bobbsey had some sort of secret.

"If you hear anything more let me know," called Bert after his sister.

"I will!" promised Nan.

The Bobbsey twins—two sets of them—had just come back from the annual summer holiday. It had been spent on the farm of Uncle Daniel Bobbsey at Meadow Brook, and while there the Bobbsey twins had visited a county fair, where they had some exciting adventures.

But summer holidays come to an end sooner or later, and this happened to the Bobbseys. They had come back to their home at Lakeport, on Lake Metoka.

"I wish we could have stayed longer," sighed Bert, as he swung in the hammock beneath the trees. "It's too hot here, and it's not the end of August! Jimminities! And school opens in about three weeks!" he added, with another deep sigh. "I wish it was about three months. I wish holidays were just beginning instead of just ending."

But still, as he thought it over and swung in the hammock, he could not help being glad that there were still three weeks more in which to have fun at the end of summer. As he had said, it was warm weather, being, in fact, the middle of August. School would open in September.

"Well, I'll get some of the fellows together and we'll see what fun we can have before school opens," said Bert, waiting for the swing of the hammock to grow less. When it came to a stop he decided he would get out and look for some of his chums, whom he had not yet seen since coming back from the county fair.

And, if Bert had only known it, there were soon to happen to him and to the other twins almost as many exciting adventures as had taken place during the early part of the holiday. Three weeks is sometimes plenty long enough for many adventures.

"I'll go and see if I can find Dannie Rugg or Charlie Mason," said Bert to himself, as he slid out of the now almost motionless hammock. "We've got to have some fun!"

Bert looked towards the house. He thought if he saw Nan he would ask her about the secret she said their father had. But, not seeing his twin sister, Bert thought there would be time enough for the secret later.

"It's too hot for anything but swimming," decided Bert. "Guess I'll get the boys and go down to the lake for a swim."

As he passed out of the garden he heard Nan singing in the kitchen where she was helping her mother get the house to rights after the holiday at Uncle Bobbsey's farm. Flossie and Freddie were still digging their "well".

"They sure do love to play in the dirt," thought Bert, as he turned down the street.

All this while Sam Johnson, the coloured man-of-all-work on the Bobbsey place, was wetting the lawn with the hose. There had been a dry spell, and the grass on the lawn was burned brown in some places. Sam was trying to bring it back to a fresh green colour by using plenty of water.

Suddenly Freddie, who had been helping Flossie scoop dirt out of the well hole, dropped his little shovel and started off.

"Where you going?" demanded Flossie.

He did not answer, but Flossie needed only one look to tell her. Sam's wife Dinah, the fat, good-natured cook, had called Sam to bring in an armful of wood, and Sam had dropped the hose, with the water still spurting from the nozzle. Freddie had seen this happen.

Losing no time, the small Bobbsey lad made a dash for the house. This was a chance not to be missed. The water was all turned on ready for him.

Freddie picked up the hose. A moment later he heard a patter of small feet behind him. It was Flossie. Freddie had hoped to sneak away all by himself and take the "squirter", as he sometimes called it. But this was not to be.

"Let me take it! I want to squirt! I want the hose!" cried Flossie.

"No!" objected Freddie, "I got it first! It's mine!"

He started to run, dragging the hose after him. He headed for the place where he and Flossie had been digging.

"I'm going to fill our well with water!" shouted Freddie.

"No, I'm going to do it! I'm going to do it!" declared Flossie.

On she ran after her brother. Freddie might have got away from her if he had not had to drag the heavy hose. But that was too much for him. It held him back.

"Let me squirt! Let me squirt!" demanded Flossie. She made a grab, trying to pull the nozzle from her brother's chubby hands. All this while the water was spurting out in a heavy stream, as Sam had the force turned on full.

As Flossie and Freddie struggled, one trying to keep and the other trying to get hold of the nozzle, you can imagine what happened. The water, instead of spurting steadily in one place, was scattered all about. Some of it even showered on the small twins.

"There! Now look what you did!" cried Flossie, as her dress became soaked.

"You did it yourself!" insisted Freddie. "Let go that nozzle! I'm going to fill my well!"

"It's as much my well as 'tis yours!" snapped back Flossie. "I want to fill it myself!"

She made a pull at the hose. The nozzle pointed up in the air. The water also went up in the air, but of course it came down again—all over Freddie.

"Now look what *you* did!" he screamed. "You're makin' me drown!"

"You did it same as I did! I'm as wet as you!" cried Flossie.

The two children were each determined to have the hose, and as they struggled and swayed to and fro, first one and then the other having hold of the nozzle, in some way it became pointed at one of the open windows of the house.

In through the windows spurted the water, and excited shouts from Dinah and Mrs. Bobbsey soon followed.

"Chilluns! Chilluns! Fo' de lan' sake, whut is yo' all doin'?" cried fat Dinah. "Good lan' ob massy! Yo' all has done gone an' drenched de' chairs an' carpet! Chilluns! Chilluns! Stop it!"

As she spoke Dinah came to the door, her fat bulk almost filling it. She saw Flossie and Freddie still struggling with the hose.

"Stop it! Stop it!" cried Dinah. "Sam, whut fo'

yo' done leave dat watah turn on when Flossie an' Freddie can git at it? Whut fo' yo' done——"

But that was all Dinah could say just then. For her mouth was suddenly filled with water from the hose. Not meaning to do it, of course, Flossie and Freddie had pointed the nozzle straight at the fat, black cook, and poor Dinah was soon drenched from the shower.

"Oh, dear!" suddenly cried Flossie, as she saw what had happened. "Look what you did, Freddie Bobbsey!" she gasped, as she let go the hose.

"You did it just as much as I did!" exclaimed Freddie, as he, too, let go the nozzle.

And then behind dripping Dinah appeared Mrs. Bobbsey, looking out at the two wet twins.

CHAPTER II

THE SECRET

MRS. BOBBSEY gave one glance at the spurting hose on the ground and then, pointing to it, she called:

"Pick it up, Freddie. Pick that hose up quickly and turn it the other way! The water is washing away my lovely dahlia flowers! Pick up the hose!"

Freddie, after ducking Dinah, had dropped the nozzle so the water was pointed in a solid stream at Mrs. Bobbsey's beautiful, large dahlia bed.

Minding what his mother had said, Freddie now picked up the hose. But he was so excited by all that had happened that he did not see what he was doing. A moment later he heard Nan cry:

"Oh, look out! You're sprinkling right through the lounge window! Stop it, Freddie!"

But Freddie did not know how to shut the water off at the nozzle and he seemed too bewildered to drop the hose. There he stood, holding it, having taken it away from the flower bed, as his mother had told him, but the water was still spraying through the open lounge window.

"Good lan' ob massy!" cried dripping Dinah. "Dis am wus dan de flood of Noah! Oh, mah lan' sakes!"

"Sam! Sam! Turn that water off!" cried Mrs. Bobbsey, as she saw Dinah's husband running across the garden, having filled the wood box as his wife had directed him. "Turn off the water!"

Sam finally managed to do that, but not before Flossie, Freddie and Dinah had been pretty well soaked, while some water was sprayed into the lounge as well as into the kitchen. However, little real damage was done, after all.

And while Dinah and Sam are mopping up after the exciting moments, and while Flossie and Freddie are putting on dry clothes, I will tell my new readers a little about the four very lively children who are to figure in this book.

* * *

As you have guessed, there were four Bobbsey twins. Bert and Nan were the older pair, but they were just as full of fun as Flossie and Freddie, the younger twins, with their fair hair and blue eyes. Bert and Nan had dark hair and eyes.

In the first book of this series, entitled *The Bobbsey Twins*, I related to you how the boys and girls lived in the eastern city of Lakeport, on Lake Metoka, where Mr. Bobbsey owned a lumber-yard. When Bert and Freddie grew up they hoped to go into the lumber business with their father. But that would not be for a long time yet.

Besides Mr. and Mrs. Bobbsey and the twins, there were Sam Johnson and his plump wife Dinah, the negro servants, who were almost members of the family. Snap, the dog, and Snoop, the cat, were also counted members of the family.

Besides having fun in their town home, playing with their school friends, the Bobbsey twins went on many trips to the country, seashore and mountains.

* * *

"And don't turn the hose on one another again," said Mrs. Bobbsey to Flossie and Freddie, as she sent them out to play after they had changed their clothes.

"We didn't do it on purpose," said Freddie. "Flossie wanted the hose and——"

"He wouldn't let me take it and I grabbed it," admitted Flossie.

"Yes, and you made a lot of trouble," said Mrs. Bobbsey. "For not only did you wet yourselves, but you splashed water indoors. So don't do it again."

"Couldn't we just take the hose to fill up our well?" begged Freddie.

"No, indeed!" laughed his mother. "If you want any water in the hole you have dug, carry it out in a pan or a pail. Leave the hose alone!"

As long as they could have some water, Flossie and Freddie were pretty well satisfied and they were soon playing again at the so-called well, trying to keep as clean and dry as possible.

Meanwhile Sam kept on watering the lawn and Mrs. Bobbsey, Nan and Dinah cleaned up, as well as they could, the water that had been showered into the house.

Just before dinner Bert came back from playing with some of his friends.

"What's all this?" he asked, when he saw Nan busy with cloths, wiping up the last of the water. "Is this the secret you were talking about?"

"No," answered Nan, turning her head so her mother wouldn't see her and putting her finger over her lips as a signal to Bert not to mention it. But Mrs. Bobbsey had heard.

"What's this about a secret?" she asked.

"Oh, Nan said father had one," replied Bert. "But——"

"What do you mean, Nan?" interrupted Mrs. Bobbsey. "What secret is it?"

"Oh, well, maybe I shouldn't have said anything," admitted Nan. "But I heard you and father talking about having to go away again, and I thought it was a secret, for I heard father tell you not to say anything about it for a while yet."

"Oh, *that!*" laughed Mrs. Bobbsey. "That isn't much of a secret."

Nan looked disappointed.

"What'd you want to go and say it was a secret for if it wasn't?" demanded Bert.

"I thought maybe we were going to have another

holiday trip," explained poor Nan. "And I thought——"

"I know you didn't mean any harm," said Mrs. Bobbsey, putting her hand on Nan's shoulder. "But it isn't wise to listen to, or hear, half a thing and then imagine the rest. It is all very simple. I know your father didn't intend it for a secret. Perhaps he will tell you about it this afternoon."

"Why don't you tell us if it isn't a secret?" asked Bert.

"Because I don't like to talk about Father's business," answered Mrs. Bobbsey.

"Oh, if it's about the lumber business I guess it isn't much of a secret," said Bert, plainly disappointed.

"Yes it is, too!" insisted Nan to her brother in a whisper, when they were out on the porch. "I heard father say there might be a lot of trouble about it."

"Trouble!" exclaimed Bert. "But what's it all about? What does it mean?"

"That's the secret part! That's what we've got to find out!" said Nan. "Maybe he'll tell us soon."

The father of the Bobbsey twins laughed when his wife told them what Nan had said about a secret.

"Well, in a way it is a secret, for I don't want everyone to know about it," admitted Mr. Bobbsey. "But I'll tell you," and he nodded to Nan.

"Won't you tell us, too?" asked Freddie. "We like secrets!"

"Yes, and you like water too, from what I hear," chuckled his father. "But all there is to the secret is this: I am having some trouble about a lot of logs I bought from a man who has a tract of timber up near Lake Melrose."

That was the next lake above Metoka, and the twins had been there once or twice.

"What sort of trouble?" asked Bert.

"I'm afraid some men are going to take away the logs I have bought," went on Mr. Bobbsey. "I wouldn't want that to happen. As soon as I heard of it I said to mother that I thought perhaps I might have to travel up to Melrose to see about it. I told her not to mention it for the present, and I suppose that's why you imagined it was a secret, Nan."

"Yes," admitted Nan, "I did."

"That's about all there is to it," went on Mr. Bobbsey. "Some men are going to try, I'm afraid, to take away my logs that I want to bring to my mill and cut up into lumber. As long as I have told you this much, I might as well tell you the rest and say that I expect to go up there next week."

"Up to Lake Melrose?" asked Mrs. Bobbsey.

"Yes," answered her husband.

"How long will you stay?"

"Oh, a week or two. Maybe three," said Mr. Bobbsey.

"Is there an hotel there where you can stay?" asked his wife.

"No, I shall have to camp out, I expect," was the answer.

"Oh! Camping out!" cried Nan and Bert together, and Bert added:

"Couldn't we camp with you?"

"Please, yes! Take us!" begged Nan. "School doesn't open for three weeks and we'd love to go!"

"We want to go camping! We want to go camping! We want to go camping!" chanted Flossie and Freddie.

"Children! Children! Please be quiet!" begged their mother. "Yes, what is it, Dinah?" she asked, for the cook appeared in the doorway of the dining-room and seemed to be trying to say something above the hub-bub.

"De telefoam am ringin' its head off," announced Dinah.

"I'll see who it is. It's probably for me," said Mr. Bobbsey.

He came back in a little while. On his face was a rather worried look, Bert thought.

"The trouble has come sooner than I expected," he said. "The men at Lake Melrose have tried to take my timber. I must go up at once and see about it."

"Oh, take us! Take us!" cried the Bobbsey twins.

CHAPTER III

FREDDIE IS CHASED

MR. BOBBSEY stood in the middle of the room, looking first at his wife and then at the eager twins. A smile replaced the worried frown on his face.

"Please take us to Lake Melrose with you!" begged Nan. "It's so hot here at the end of summer. And we have more than three weeks yet until school holidays are over."

"We could have a lot of fun at Lake Melrose," said Bert softly.

"And I could go swimmin'!" added Freddie, quickly.

"And fishin'!" put in Flossie.

"You seem to have pretty good arguments, children," said Mr. Bobbsey. "What do you say, Mother?" he asked his wife.

"Do you really have to go up there?" she inquired.

"I really ought to," was the answer. "The sooner I can get the timber shipped down here the better. Now, children, please be quiet a moment," begged

Mr. Bobbsey, for he saw that the twins were getting ready to start teasing to be taken on another trip. "I must think about this, and in a moment or two perhaps I'll tell you what I am going to do."

Mr. Bobbsey went back to the telephone to call up his office and speak to some of his men. Meanwhile Freddie and Flossie talked in excited whispers of what they would do if they could go to Lake Melrose. Bert and Nan recalled the time they had once gone on a picnic there.

Lake Melrose joined Lake Metoka by a small river, and rafts of logs could easily be floated from one lake to the other. Once they were in Lake Metoka they could be towed to Mr. Bobbsey's mill and sawed into boards.

Presently Mr. Bobbsey returned from the telephone. He seemed to have made up his mind. The children waited for their father to speak.

"Well," he said, "I have decided. It is best that I go to Lake Melrose as soon as possible to save my timber from being taken by men who have no right to it. And as there is no school I suppose I'll take you children along."

"Hurray!" cried Nan and Bert.

"Goodie! Goodie!" shouted Flossie and Freddie.

"So, Mother," went on Mr. Bobbsey, smiling at his wife, "if it isn't too much trouble for you to get ready to go off on another trip, we'll do it."

"Oh, it isn't really any trouble," said Mrs. Bobbsey slowly. "We have only just started to open the house, and Sam and Dinah can close it again."

"When can we go?" asked Bert. He was impatient to start.

"Tomorrow," answered his father. "There isn't really much to do to get ready, as it isn't a very long journey. We'll go in the car, and take enough to stay about three weeks."

"Where shall we stay?" asked Nan. "In a tent?"

"There's a house at Lake Melrose—a bungalow," her father replied. "It isn't a very good one—more like a tumble-down shack than anything else—but I think it will shelter us for the time we need it. We are likely to have good weather, I think.

"Now, Mother," he added, as he looked for his hat, "I must get back to the office right away. I'll leave it to you to make all the arrangements, and we'll start for Lake Melrose in the car as early as possible in the morning."

"Goodie! Goodie!" shrieked the children.

Then Mr. Bobbsey hurried off, leaving the twins so excited they hardly knew what to do. The prospect of another journey, coming so soon after the exciting adventures at the county fair, was almost too much for them. Freddie actually stood on his head; and Flossie tried hard to do the same, but did not quite succeed.

"We'll help you get ready," offered Nan. "Won't we, Bert?"

"Yes," he answered.

"I think I shall need your help," said Mrs. Bobbsey. "Two holidays in the same summer is a little more than I counted on."

But the Bobbsey family was one that often made unexpected journeys and so it did not take very long to get ready for this one. Not many supplies needed to be taken along, as food and other things could be bought at Lake Melrose. So after the clothing had been packed and Sam and Dinah had been told to look after matters until the family returned, about all there was to do was to wait until next day.

"Is dey any hoses up by dat lake?" asked Dinah the next morning, when they were waiting for Mr. Bobbsey to bring the car round to the door.

"Hoses?" questioned Nan. "Do you mean horses, Dinah?"

"No, honey lamb, Ah means *hoses*—hoses whut squirt water," and she looked at Flossie and Freddie and laughed until her fat sides shook.

"Oh, that!" cried Nan. "No, I guess there aren't any hose lines up there, Dinah, for Flossie and Freddie to play with," and the smaller twins chuckled as they remembered what had happened.

"Here comes Daddy! Here comes Daddy!" cried Freddie, as he caught the sound of an approaching car.

Instantly there was a buzz of excitement, which was only quieted when the family was seated in the car, their baggage around them, and on the way to camp at Lake Melrose. Dinah and Sam stood at the gate waving their hands in farewell. Snap, the dog, barked his good-byes, and Snoop, the fat cat, rubbed up against Dinah's legs, for this was a way of begging milk.

Flossie and Freddie wanted to take the cat and the dog with them, but their father said the animals would be in the way and might get lost in the woods. This last idea did more than any other to make the smaller twins agree to let Snoop and Snap remain at home.

It was a fine day. The sun shone brightly, almost too brightly in fact, for it was very warm, but the speed of the car brought a welcome breeze. Mr. and Mrs. Bobbsey sat in the front seat, talking together, and the four twins were in the back.

They had travelled several miles along the shore of Lake Metoka and Mr. Bobbsey had just pointed out to his wife a pretty scene along the road when suddenly there was a loud noise like the pop of a gun.

"What's that?" sharply cried Mr. Bobbsey. "A flat tyre?"

He slowed down the car and steered to the side of the road, but laughter from the twins in the rear seat soon made him understand that nothing serious had happened.

"It was my balloon," said Freddie. "It broke!"

"He blew it too big!" added Flossie. "Now I can't blow it, and he said I could! What'd you want to go and burst it for?" she asked, rather crossly.

"I—I didn't mean to do it," announced Freddie. He had brought with him a toy red rubber balloon, and had been amusing himself by blowing it full of air and watching it grow smaller as he let the air out. But he had blown once too often and the balloon had "popped".

"Have you another balloon?" asked Mr. Bobbsey, as he started the car again.

"No," answered Freddie, looking at the limp shreds of his plaything. "But you can stop and buy me one at the next town if you want to, Daddy," he said.

"Ho! I don't believe I want to!" laughed Mr. Bobbsey. "It was rather a scare you gave me as it was—making me think a tyre had blown out. No more balloons, Freddie, until we get where we're going."

"And then it's my turn to have one," insisted Flossie.

"Maybe," said her father, with a smile at Mrs. Bobbsey.

Mrs. Bobbsey had put up a lunch to take with them in the car, and when noon came the car was stopped beneath some trees at the side of the road and boxes and baskets were opened.

"It's lots of fun to eat this way," said Nan, as she helped her mother pass the sandwiches.

"Like a picnic," agreed Bert. "I'd always rather eat this way than at a table."

"It saves washing dishes, at any rate," observed Mrs. Bobbsey.

Flossie and Freddie always managed to finish their lunch first, and this time it was the same. They brushed the crumbs from their laps and asked if they could not get out of the car and run around. Knowing that little legs get cramped if kept still too long, Mrs. Bobbsey let the smaller twins get out of the car.

"Don't go too far away," she cautioned them, and they promised not to.

For a time Mrs. Bobbsey and Nan were so busy putting away the remains of the lunch, while Bert and his father tightened a loose bolt on the car, that none of them paid any attention to Flossie and Freddie. The first they knew that anything was wrong was when Flossie came running down the road, her hair flying in the wind and her blue eyes gleaming with excitement as she cried:

"Oh, it's after Freddie! It's after Freddie!"

"What is?" asked her mother, as, above Flossie's cries, could be heard the frightened shouts of the little boy. "Who's after Freddie, Flossie?" asked Mrs. Bobbsey.

"A big sheep!" was the answer. "He's got horns!"

A moment later Freddie came into view, racing around the turn in the road, and behind the boy came a leaping ram, with big, curved horns.

"Daddy! Mother!" howled Freddie. "Catch him! Save me!"

CHAPTER IV

ANGRY MEN

THERE was no time to ask how it happened that the ram, or sheep, as Flossie called the animal, had come to chase Freddie. Something must be done right away to save the little boy from the horns of the angry ram. For the ram was angry, of that there was no doubt.

On it raced after Freddie, now and then bleating loudly. Freddie shouted again and again:

"Save me! Help me! Daddy! Mother! Help me!"

Mr. Bobbsey dived out from under the car where he and Bert had been tightening one of the nuts.

"Freddie!" cried Mrs. Bobbsey, flinging open the car door. "What *have* you been up to this time?"

"Throw something at it!" cried Nan, and she threw an empty lunch box. But as this was very light it did not go far. And even if it had hit the ram it would not have stopped him.

Luckily Freddie was a good runner, but, good as

he was, he could not have kept up the race much longer and have held his place in front of the ram. All the while the angry animal, with his big, curved horns, was coming nearer and nearer.

Bert leaped out and threw a spanner at the ram. It hit him in the side with a thump, and made him grunt, Bert said afterwards. It could not have hurt the ram very much, for the animal was big and fat and his sides were covered with thick pads of wool.

But being hit with the spanner made the ram turn a little to one side, so, instead of racing directly after Freddie, he pounded on directly towards the back of the car at one side of the road.

Seeing this Nan cried:

"Turn off, Freddie! Turn off! Let him pass you!"

Freddie heard and obeyed. He swerved to the right and the ram, whose big head was lowered so that he could butt the little boy, did not see where he was going to hit. The Bobbseys did, however, all but Freddie.

"Oh, that ram is going to run into our car!" cried Nan, for the beast was headed straight for the back of the car. "He's going to run into us!" Nan shouted. "Did you ever!"

"Let him!" advised Bert, with a laugh, for he saw that Freddie would soon be out of danger. "He can't hurt the car—it's harder than he is!"

"Gracious!" screamed Nan.

A moment later with a crash that could be heard a

long way off, the ram butted into the spring bumper at the back of Mr. Bobbsey's car. The spring bent in a little and then, bouncing out, threw the ram back. The angry animal was tossed back so hard that he fell down in the dust of the road with a loud bleat of pain and amazement.

For several seconds the ram lay there, so surprised and shaken by the shock that he did not seem to know what had happened. By this time Mrs. Bobbsey had climbed down out of the car and had lifted Freddie into it, while Bert gathered up Flossie, who had climbed to the running-board on the side to be out of danger.

"What did you do, Freddie, to make the ram chase you?" asked his mother.

"Nothing," Freddie answered, when he was breathing more slowly, for he was out of breath from his long run. "I just opened the gate to his field to go in and pick some flowers for you and he came out at me."

"You shouldn't have opened the gate," said Mr. Bobbsey. "This is evidently an ugly ram and we are going to have trouble with him, I'm afraid."

"He's getting up," said Mrs. Bobbsey, looking at the ram that was now struggling in the dust of the road. "Get a stick or something, Dick," she said to her husband, "and chase him away."

"I'll get that spanner," said Bert, starting towards the tool that he had thrown. He could see it where it had fallen at the side of the road.

"No, don't go near him!" cried Nan.

"Oh, is he coming after me again?" half sobbed Freddie.

But the ram had, very plainly, had enough of bumping into a heavy vehicle, especially on a spring bumper. The animal staggered to its feet, shook its head as though to get rid of a dizzy feeling and then, with one look at the car and a stamp of its front feet, turned and marched off down the road.

"I guess he had enough!" laughed Bert. "That was some bump he got!"

"He doesn't seem to care to be any better acquainted with us," agreed Mr. Bobbsey, with a smile.

Down the road came running a farmer. He stopped as he caught sight of the ram and seemed afraid.

"Did he make trouble for you?" the farmer called to Mr. Bobbsey. "I don't see how he got out of the pasture. I keep him barred in, for he's an ugly ram. He goes for me sometimes."

"My little boy opened the gate, not knowing about the ram," said Mr. Bobbsey. "But I think his temper is gone for a time. He ran into our car full tilt."

"And he knocked himself down!" added Flossie.

"Served him right!" laughed the farmer. "Well, I'm glad nobody was hurt. Get along there, you old Ebenezer!" he cried. "The stuffing seems to be taken all out of you," he added. And truly the ram did not even shake his head at the farmer, but marched slowly along the road and meekly allowed himself to be driven back to the pasture.

"You mustn't open any more farm gates, not even

to pick flowers for me, Freddie," said Mrs. Bobbsey, when they were ready to travel on again. "The next time a bull might chase you, and a bull is a great deal worse than a ram."

"I told him not to open the gate, but he did," said Flossie. "I saw the sheep with the big horns, but Freddie said he wouldn't do anything to us."

"He didn't do anything," insisted Freddie. "And he didn't hurt the car at all, did he, Daddy?"

"No. But there might have been an accident," said Mr. Bobbsey. "Mind your mother and don't open any more farm gates."

"I won't," promised Freddie, who had received a good fright—that is, it was a good fright in that it would keep him from doing that same sort of mischief again.

"Moreover, it was not right to put the farmer to the trouble of looking for his ram," added Mr. Bobbsey.

"Pick up the spanner, Bert, and we'll get on our way," called Mr. Bobbsey to his elder son. "I want to reach Lake Melrose before dark so that we can get the old bungalow partly to rights."

"Oh, I just know we're going to have a lovely time camping there!" exclaimed Nan happily.

"And I hope we have some adventures," remarked Bert, as he put the spanner back in the tool box.

About three o'clock, when still several miles from Lake Melrose, as they were driving along a quiet country road, there was a sudden hiss from one of the rear tyres.

"We've run over a snake!" cried Nan. "I heard it hiss."

"More likely it's a puncture!" laughed Mr. Bobbsey, and so it proved. The right rear tyre was as "flat as a pancake", as Bert expressed it.

But as two spare wheels, fully blown up, were carried, it was not much of a task to make the change. While Mr. Bobbsey jacked up the car and prepared to put the good tyre on in place of the flat one, Bert standing by to help all he could, Nan with her mother and the smaller twins walked down the road towards a distant farmhouse. They wanted to ask for a drink of water.

"Wouldn't the children like some nice milk?" asked the farmer's wife, when she had said they would be welcome to drinks of water.

"I like milk," announced Flossie.

"So do I, and cookies too. Dinah, at home, gives us milk and cookies," explained Freddie, as if afraid the farm woman might not understand.

"So Dinah gives you milk and cookies, does she?" laughed the woman. "Well, my name isn't Dinah, but I have plenty of milk and a jar of molasses cookies I just baked. May I give them some?" she asked Mrs. Bobbsey, smiling sweetly.

"I'm afraid it's too much trouble. It is very kind of you, but——"

"No trouble at all. Please come in," and into the pleasant farmhouse they went. Mrs. Bobbsey admitted that she, too, was hungry enough to wish a glass of milk and some of the brown cookies, and when they were being served Freddie looked closely at the kind woman and remarked:

"Your name couldn't be Dinah, anyhow!"

"No? Couldn't it, little boy? Why not?"

"'Cause Dinah's black an' you're white," was the answer, as the others laughed. "But she doesn't bake any better cookies than you do," added Freddie, with generous praise.

"I'm glad you like them," said Mrs. Benton, which was the name of the farmer's wife. And she was so good-natured that she insisted on Mr. Bobbsey and Bert coming in to wash their hands, after changing the wheel. Then she gave them some milk and cookies, and Mr. Bobbsey said it was one of the best lunches he had ever eaten.

"Changing wheels always gives me an appetite," he explained.

"This was a good place to get an appetite," remarked Mrs. Bobbsey with a laugh, as she thanked Mrs. Benton.

The Bobbsey twins were soon on their way again, and in another half-hour they reached Lake Melrose.

"This is a nice place," said Freddie, as he glanced around the shores of the beautiful lake.

"You s'pose maybe there's any sheep here with big horns?" asked Flossie, who was still thinking of the ram that had chased her twin brother.

"No, I hardly think there's any around here," said her father, with a laugh. "Our bungalow is in rather a wild part of the woods, though I think there is a farmhouse about a mile away where we can get things to eat," he added to his wife.

A road, not a very good one, but a road they could travel over in the car, led around the lake, and along this Mr. Bobbsey drove until they came within sight of what had once been a fine bungalow on the shore.

But now the bungalow was pretty much in ruins, though, as Mr. Bobbsey said, it would shelter them for a week or two, as they would be out of doors most of the time, only sleeping inside.

"The kitchen is in pretty fair shape," said Mrs. Bobbsey, after a visit to it. "We can do very well here, and it certainly is a lovely place and much cooler than Lakeport would be at this time of year."

"Well, do the best you can," suggested Mr. Bobbsey. "I wouldn't have come up here except for the trouble over the timber."

"Where is your timber?" asked Bert, when he had finished helping carry the things into the bungalow.

"Stacked over there," and Mr. Bobbsey pointed to a big pile of logs near the shore of the lake, not far from the camp. As he spoke Mr. Bobbsey looked more sharply at the timber and Bert, following his father's gaze, saw a number of roughly dressed men walking around the logs.

"I must see what those men want," remarked Mr. Bobbsey. "I haven't yet hired the men who are to ship the logs to my mill."

Bert followed his father towards the pile of timber. As Mr. Bobbsey approached, the group of rough men stood together, waiting for Mr. Bobbsey to take some action.

"What are you doing here?" asked Mr. Bobbsey of the men.

"Looking after our timber," was the answer of one, who seemed to be a sort of foreman.

"Your timber!" cried Mr. Bobbsey. "These logs are mine! And I wish you to go away from here!"

"We'll go when our claim is settled," said one man, in a surly voice.

"What claim do you mean?" asked the father of the twins.

"Our claim for cutting and stacking this lumber," was the answer. "We haven't been paid yet, and this timber doesn't get away from here until we get our money."

"I don't owe you any money," said Mr. Bobbsey.

"Somebody does," declared the man. "What's your name?" he suddenly asked.

"Bobbsey—Richard Bobbsey," answered Bert's father.

"That's the name! That's the man who owes us money!" cried the other men in angry tones.

"Yes, that's the name all right," said the leader. "Bobbsey is what he called himself. Well, Mr. Bobbsey," the fellow went on, "my name is Rawlin, Hank Rawlin, and this is my gang of wood choppers. You owe us money and you've got to pay us," and he shook his fist at Bert's father.

"Look here, my man," said Mr. Bobbsey quietly. "I don't know you, and I don't know your men. I don't owe you any money, but I do own this timber and I'm going to send it down to Lake Metoka where I have a mill. I don't want any trouble with you, but I'm not afraid of you, and I want you to leave my ground, for I have rented this tract until I get my timber off it."

"Don't let him scare you, Hank!" cried some of the other men. "We want our money!"

"Yes, and we're going to get it!" threatened Hank Rawlin. "Not a stick of this timber do you move until you pay us!" he cried, walking close to Mr. Bobbsey and shaking his fist so angrily that Bert caught up a stick and hurried to his father's side.

CHAPTER V

FREDDIE'S BIG FISH

THOUGH the lumber men seemed very angry, as doubtless they were on account of not getting their money, Mr. Bobbsey was not at all angry, nor did he seem afraid. Bert was glad of this, for he knew that in a fight he and his father could not do much against six or seven men.

"Now look here, Rawlin," said Mr. Bobbsey in even tones, "there must be some mistake. I didn't hire you to cut this timber, and if I had hired you I would have paid you. I'm not in the habit of cheating men who work for me. Did you ever see me before?"

"No, I don't know's I did," admitted Hank, as he picked a bit of bark from one of the piled logs. "But maybe some of my men did. Any of you ever see Mr. Bobbsey before?" he asked, turning to the wood choppers behind him.

"No, I didn't," said one.

"Not that I know of," answered another, shaking his head.

"I don't remember his face," replied a third slowly.

"Well, even if we didn't ever see you before," went on Hank, "somebody who spoke for you hired us to cut and stack this timber, and they said you'd pay us. Now we want to be paid!" His voice was angry again.

"I tell you there must be some mistake!" declared Mr. Bobbsey. "I never hired anyone to cut this timber, for I bought it after it was cut down. I bought it from a man named Kling."

Hank Rawlin shook his big head and grizzled beard.

"The man who hired us was named Bobbsey," he insisted. "And as you say that's your name you've got to pay us the money or else not a stick can be moved."

"That's right!" chimed in the other men one after another.

Mr. Bobbsey was getting a little provoked now.

"I tell you there is a big mistake somewhere," he said. "I never hired you nor saw you before. If you never saw me before how can you say that I hired you to cut these trees down and pile them here?"

"It was a man named Waydell who hired us, and he said Mr. Bobbsey would pay us," said Hank.

Bert's father shook his head.

"There's a mistake somewhere," he went on. "Now I'll tell you what you'd better do," he went on. "Bring this man Waydell here and I'll soon prove that I never told him to hire you nor did I promise him that I would pay you. Bring this man Waydell to see me."

"Yes, and while we're gone you'll ship away the logs and how'll we get our money?" asked Hank.

"These logs won't be shipped for several days yet," promised Mr. Bobbsey. "I have to hire men to make them up into rafts and float them down to Lake Metoka. I am here with my family, and I'm going to stay for two weeks or more. You needn't be afraid that I'll run off with the lumber in the night, though the logs are mine to do with as I please. But you can safely leave here to go after Waydell. He's the man I want to see if he said I promised to pay you."

"Well, maybe that's fair," admitted Hank, in a growling voice. "But if anyone tries to cheat us out of our money it will go hard with him! Eh, fellows?"

"That's right!" cried the lumbermen. "Let's go get Waydell!"

And off through the woods the men went while Mr. Bobbsey, watching them, shook his head in a puzzled way. He could not understand what it all meant.

"Do you think there'll be trouble?" asked Bert of his father, as he dropped the stick, for which he saw no further use. Very likely he would not have been allowed to strike with it anyhow.

"Yes, it does look as though there might be trouble over this timber," admitted Mr. Bobbsey. "But it isn't my fault. I didn't hire those men nor promise to pay them. I bought the timber, as it is piled, from Kling, and he never said there was any money owing the cutters. I expect it will come out all right. Don't worry, Bert. You're here to have a good time. I'll take care of that crowd of lumbermen."

Bert trusted his father. He knew that Mr. Bobbsey knew how to manage lumber deals, so the boy was soon thinking more of the good times in store than about the fuss over the timber.

"What did those men want?" asked Mrs. Bobbsey, when her husband and Bert returned to the bungalow, which was being put to rights.

Mr. Bobbsey told her and also advised her not to worry, as he would straighten everything out.

But, in spite of this, Nan and Bert could not help thinking that trouble might come to their father from the angry men led by Hank Rawlin.

"Suppose they came in the night and took away the logs," said Nan to Bert. "Wouldn't that be awful?"

"If they did we'd hear them and get up and make them stop," was Bert's answer.

"You and Dad aren't enough to stop six or seven men," said Nan.

"Well, then we'll send down to the lumber-yard and get men to help us," Bert declared. "You leave it to Dad!"

"Yes, I guess we'll have to," sighed Nan. "But it's too bad it happened."

Flossie and Freddie were too small to understand anything about business troubles. They loved to roam in the woods and play about the shore of the lake and they felt sure there were going to be many happy days of this kind for them.

There were several busy hours spent in getting ready for the night, arranging the beds in the old bungalow and preparing to cook supper and arrange for breakfast. But the Bobbseys were used to camping out, and that is what they were now doing, though they were in a log bungalow instead of in a tent. But the tent was to come later, as my readers shall see.

In the evening, when supper had been served, the children being allowed to roast potatoes in a fire outside the bungalow, and when the dishes had been put away and the bunks made, the family sat in front of the "shack", as Mr. Bobbsey called it, talking over the events of the day.

They laughed at Freddie's "rambunctious time", as they called his flight before the old ram, and spoke with pleasure of the lunch of milk and molasses cookies that the kind farmer's wife had given them.

"Daddy, you s'pose there's any fish in this lake?" asked Freddie, after a pause, during which Flossie had yawned sleepily several times.

"Oh, yes, Freddie, I suppose there are as many fish in this lake as in ours at home," answered Mr. Bobbsey. "In a way the two lakes are almost like one, being joined by the river."

"Well, I'm going fishing tomorrow," decided Freddie.

"All right. But I think the place for you to go now is bed," replied his mother. "And Flossie, too."

The smaller twins were tucked in their bunks, and soon Bert and Nan went to their rooms.

"Do you think those angry lumbermen might come

in the night and make trouble?" asked Mrs. Bobbsey, in a low voice to her husband as they were locking up the bungalow.

"I hardly think so," he answered. "They know I won't take the logs away in the night, and they can't very well work after dark. They would make too much noise—we'd hear them."

"I wish we'd brought our dog along," said Mrs. Bobbsey, with a nervous look at the windows.

"Don't worry," laughed her husband. "Everything will be all right, I'm sure. So don't worry."

But in spite of this Mrs. Bobbsey did worry. Several times she imagined she heard queer noises and she awakened her husband.

"It's only the wind," he said, and so it proved.

But, towards morning, there was really a loud noise. Someone was heard walking about in the living-room of the bungalow.

"Richard! Dick! Wake up!" whispered his wife, shaking him. "Someone is in the house!"

"That's right! Someone is out there!" agreed Mr. Bobbsey, as he listened to footsteps in the other room. He put on a robe and slippers and opened the door. Mrs. Bobbsey heard him laugh. Then she heard him call out:

"What's the matter, Freddie? Why are you out of bed?"

"Oh! Oh!" gasped the voice of the little boy. "I want to catch a fish! I got to catch a fish!"

"Freddie, you're walking and talking in your sleep!" said his father, as he caught him up in his arms and carried him back into the room which he shared with Flossie.

And that's just what Freddie had been doing. He was thinking so much about going fishing the next day that it entered into his dreams, and he got up, while still asleep, and wandered out into the living-room.

He hardly awakened as his father picked him up and put him back in bed, and the next morning Freddie hardly believed it when they told him what had happened. He did not remember a thing about it.

"Next time I want to walk with you," said Flossie.

"There mustn't be any next time," laughed Mrs. Bobbsey.

The fine weather continued, and the Bobbseys, after a breakfast in the bungalow, made ready to spend a happy time in the woods and on the lake. There were some boats tied to a wharf in front of the old bungalow, and after promising to be careful, Freddie and Flossie were allowed to go in one of these and paddle out, not too far from shore, while Freddie tried his luck at fishing.

Mr. Bobbsey was busy taking an account of his logs to see how many there were in the big pile, so he would know how many rafts to make to float them down to his lumber mill. Bert went with his father to help, and Nan and Mrs. Bobbsey began to get the bungalow more to rights.

Bert and Mr. Bobbsey were out of sight behind the big pile of logs, and Nan had come to the door to empty a dustpan of dirt that she had swept up, when suddenly from the boat from which Flossie and Freddie were fishing came a cry of fear.

"Oh, quick! Quick!" screamed Flossie. "Freddie's caught a big fish and it's pulling him into the lake! Hurry!"

CHAPTER VI

BERT IS CAUGHT

NAN dropped the dustpan and sprang towards the water's edge. As she ran she cried:

"Freddie! Freddie! Sit still! Look out or you'll fall overboard!"

Well might she say this, for her small brother was leaning far over the edge of the boat, holding fast to his rod. The line was stretched out tight, and was cutting through the water, first this way and then that, as though some big fish had hold of the hook.

Flossie was leaning back as far as she could on the other side of the boat, for the small twins had been on the water often enough to know how best to prevent a boat from tipping over. Flossie was not going to have an upset if she could help it.

"What has happened?" called Mrs. Bobbsey, running to the door as she heard the clatter of the falling dustpan and Nan's cry. Then she saw the dangerous position of Freddie in the boat and ran towards him as Nan had done.

By this time Bert and Mr. Bobbsey, at the timber pile, also heard the cries and knew that something was wrong. They came running around the corner of the pile of logs, and no sooner had Mr. Bobbsey seen the danger of his little son than he ran to another boat that was tied to the small dock and began rowing out towards Flossie and Freddie.

"Oh, Daddy! Come quick! Come quick!" screamed

Flossie, even though her father was rowing as fast as he could. "The big fish will get Freddie!"

"Freddie! Freddie!" called his father. "Lean back in the boat and let go of your rod!" For Mr. Bobbsey could see that Freddie was merely holding to the rod with his hands—the line was not entangled around the little fellow—and if he let go all danger would be over.

But Freddie did not want to let go. He felt sure he had caught a big fish—the largest in the lake, perhaps—and he did not want to lose his prize. So his chubby hands kept firm hold of the rod, which bent this way and that as the tight line zigzagged through the water, swishing this way and that as something on the other end pulled hard.

"Freddie! Freddie! Let go!" called his mother.

"I—don't—want to—lose—my—fish!" shouted Freddie, his breath and words coming in gasps, for it was hard work to talk and keep hold of his rod.

"He must have caught a lake trout," said Bert, as he joined his mother and sister at the edge of the water, while his father was quickly rowing out to the small twins in their boat. "That's the biggest fish in the lake, but they hardly ever catch 'em until cold weather."

"Oh, Freddie is always doing something different!" exclaimed Nan. They were not so frightened now, for Mr. Bobbsey was close to Flossie and her brother in his boat, and, even if Freddie should upset or fall overboard, his father could now rescue him.

"What in the world have you caught, Freddie?" cried Mr. Bobbsey, as his boat rubbed up alongside the fishing craft. "Here, let me get hold of your line!"

"No, I want to pull it in myself!" insisted Freddie, no longer frightened now that his father was beside him. Flossie, too, had stopped her cries for help.

"Well, pull it in then," answered the twins' father, for he believed in letting children do things for themselves.

Freddie tried again to lift his rod up high enough to bring with it whatever was hooked on the other end of the line, for he did not have a reel on which the line could be wound in. But as he raised his rod it bent so nearly double that his father cried:

"Look out, Freddie, or it will break!"

"That's what I'm 'fraid of," Freddie said. "Else I could pull this fish in myself."

"Well, you certainly have something very lively on your hook," remarked Mr. Bobbsey. The line was still swishing back and forth in the water, but whatever was on the hook could not be seen. "Hold still a minute now and I'll get hold of the line and pull it in that way," said Mr. Bobbsey. "The line won't break as quickly as the rod will."

He reached over from his boat and caught hold of Freddie's line. As he pulled, the thing beneath the water tried hard to swim away, but Mr. Bobbsey had a firm hold and kept on drawing in.

"Oh, I see it! I see it!" cried Flossie, leaning over the side of the boat.

"Flossie! Keep back or you'll fall in!" warned her mother.

A moment later Mr. Bobbsey lifted from the water a large, black round object like a dishpan. It was the colour of tar, and it was fastened to the line by a long, snake-like neck and a small but ugly head with jaws almost like a parrot's beak.

"It's a big snapping turtle!" cried Bert, when he saw the object.

"That's what it is," said Mr. Bobbsey, as he raised the turtle farther from the water. "You don't want this, Freddie. It isn't a fish at all."

"Yes, I do want it!" cried Freddie. "I caught it and

it's mine! I want it! I'm going to make a pen and keep it!"

"He'll bite," announced Flossie. And indeed the turtle very likely would have done that if it could have found anything to bite on, for its jaws were opening and closing as Mr. Bobbsey raised it from the water, and the snake-like eyes seemed to glitter in anger.

"Are you going to let him bring that horrid creature here?" asked Mrs. Bobbsey.

"Yes, I want him!" cried Freddie, making a grab for the line that his father still held. "I caught him and I want him, even if he isn't any fish! I want him!"

But the turtle solved the question for itself. With a hard snap of its jaws it cut the line close to where it entered its mouth and dropped back into the water with a large splash.

"There he goes!" cried Flossie.

"Oh, he's gone—my nice big mud turtle!" sighed Freddie.

"He wasn't nice—he was nasty!" declared Flossie.

"And it wasn't a mud turtle. It was a snapping turtle and might have bitten you," went on Mr. Bobbsey.

"Oh, would he? Then I don't want him," said Freddie. "I'm glad he's gone," and he leaned over the boat to catch a glimpse of the turtle. But the creature had disappeared beneath the water.

"You might just as well be glad as sorry," laughed Mr. Bobbsey, as he rowed back towards shore, followed by the small twins. "How did you come to catch it, Freddie?"

"He caught himself," Freddie answered. "Flossie and I were fishing for fish, and I felt something pull hard on my line, so I pulled in."

"And he 'most pulled Freddie into the water," added Flossie.

"But I held on!" exclaimed Freddie.

"Yes, but sometimes it's better to let go," warned his father. "I didn't think there were in the lake large enough fish to pull like that."

"Lake trout might," suggested Bert, as he helped Flossie and Freddie to make their boat fast to the dock.

"Yes," agreed Mr. Bobbsey. "But lake trout don't bite at this time of the year, and they wouldn't be likely to take the hook or the bait Freddie was using. Besides, the trout are only in the deeper part of the lake. But until I saw the turtle I couldn't guess what it was that Freddie had hooked."

"I was afraid he'd go overboard," remarked Mrs. Bobbsey. "Do be careful after this, Freddie."

"I will," promised the blue-eyed little fellow. "But I couldn't help the turtle taking hold of my hook, could I?"

"No," agreed Mrs. Bobbsey, with a smile. "I don't suppose you could. But now play on shore for a while."

This the small twins did, while Bert and his father went back to the pile of logs and Nan and her mother worked in the bungalow. Every now and then, as Flossie and Freddie played on the shore of Lake

Melrose, the little boy would look out across the water toward the place where he had been fishing, and he would say:

"It was an awful big turtle! I wish I had him!"

"I don't!" exclaimed Flossie. "He might bite. Daddy said so!"

"Not if he was in a cage like a lion at the circus," said Freddie.

"Oh, well, you haven't got him, anyhow," ended Flossie.

The day passed without any return of the men who claimed that Mr. Bobbsey owed them money for cutting logs, and Mrs. Bobbsey hoped they would not come back to make trouble. Mr. Bobbsey said he would get the police, if necessary, to keep the men away, as he knew they had no claim on him.

The Bobbsey twins were delighted to be again in the woods and camping at the lake, and they planned many days of fun, for Mr. Bobbsey had said it would take two weeks or more to get all the logs floated down to Lake Metoka and to his mill.

On the third day of their stay at the Lake Melrose bungalow, Mr. Bobbsey started off for the nearest town as soon as breakfast was over. He said he wanted to hire some men to put the logs into the lake.

"You look after things while I'm gone, Bert," said Mr. Bobbsey to his elder boy. "And if Rawlin and his men come back don't interfere with them nor talk to them."

"But supposing they take your logs, Dad?"

"I don't think they will, but let them. They can't

get away with very many before I'll be back. And I'll stop them—don't you try."

"All right," agreed Bert, but he rather felt that if he had the chance he could protect his father's timber.

After Mr. Bobbsey had been gone some time, and while Mrs. Bobbsey was amusing the small twins by playing a game with them, Bert called to Nan.

"Come on out into the woods a little way."

"What are you going to do?" asked Nan.

Bert made sure his mother could not hear him before he answered:

"I'm going to make a trap to catch a bear!"

"Oh!" exclaimed Nan, with a delicious thrill of fear and delight. "I'll help you."

Bert had some idea of how a bear trap is made of heavy logs in the form of a pen in which bruin is caught alive. He had seen a picture of such a trap in one of his father's books. With the help of Nan the boy began to build the trap. He had heard it said there were bears in the woods around Lake Melrose, though Bert hardly hoped any of the animals would come around before cold weather set in, when they would be hungry because all the fruit and berries would be gone.

"But we'll make a trap, anyhow," said Bert to his sister, "and maybe we'll catch a bear in it after we go back home."

"What good will that do?" Nan asked

"Maybe dad and I will come back here to see about the timber or something, and then we can get the bear," Bert explained.

So the trap was started. There were plenty of small logs lying about in the woods—logs too small for the lumbermen to care about—and these Bert and Nan piled into what Bert thought was the proper form of trap. Afterwards he knew it was not the right kind of trap at all, and that no bear ever could have been caught in it. But, at the time, Nan and Bert thought it was just the best bear trap ever made.

And it did catch something. I'll say that for it.

The logs had been piled into a pen-shaped structure and Bert was arranging several heavy sticks in the form of a door, to fall and close the opening when the bear should walk in and take the bait, when all at once something slipped.

There was a rumble and clatter of falling logs. Bert heard them, but not in time. He tried to spring clear, and cried to Nan:

"Look out!"

Nan was out of danger, but Bert was fairly caught in his own bear trap. The logs fell on and around him, pinning him down. He gave a cry of alarm and pain, shouting:

"Oh, Nan! Nan! Get mother or somebody! I'm caught!"

CHAPTER VII

FLOSSIE'S PIE

NAN BOBBSEY had been frightened when she heard the rumble and crash of falling logs from Bert's bear trap. But she was much more frightened when she heard her brother cry out and ask her to go for help.

"Are you much hurt, Bert?" asked Nan, nearly crying.

"Well, maybe not so much—yet," he answered. "I don't believe my arms or legs are broken. But I'm held down. I can't move or get out. The logs are all criss-crossed round me like jack-straws."

And that is the best way of telling you how Bert was caught. It was exactly like the jack-straws you let fall in a heap on the table when you play that game. The logs were piled "every which way" around the boy who was in the midst of them.

No logs, or, at any rate, only a few of them, had actually fallen on Bert's body or limbs. But he was penned in the trap even more securely than a big black bear would have been caught.

"You'd better go for mother!" called Bert, and Nan sped away. Both she and her brother wished their father was at home, but Mr. Bobbsey had gone away to see about his lumber helpers.

"Mother! Mother!" shouted Nan, as she reached the bungalow, in front of which Mrs. Bobbsey sat reading a story to Flossie and Freddie. "Oh, Mother, Bert is caught in the bear trap!"

"He is?" cried Mrs. Bobbsey, getting to her feet and dropping the book. "Where? Take me to him, Nan. Quickly, dear."

"Is the bear there?" asked Flossie in frightened tones.

"If he is I want to see him!" declared Freddie.

"There isn't any bear!" answered Nan. "Bert is caught in the logs he was making the trap with!"

"Is he much hurt?" asked Mrs. Bobbsey, as she sped along the woodland path after her daughter.

"No, I guess he isn't hurt much," Nan said. "But he can't get out unless we raise the logs off him."

"If your father were only here!" murmured the children's mother.

As they neared the place where Bert had started to build the bear trap the boy's voice could be heard calling:

"Hurry up! Hurry up, somebody! I want to get out!"

"We're coming!" called his mother. "Don't be afraid, Bert. We're coming!"

Mrs. Bobbsey looked at the tangled mass of logs, beneath which Bert was pinned. She did not stop to ask why Bert had done it, though the boy himself now realized that it was very wrong of him to try to build so heavy a trap alone, or only with Nan's help. Instead of asking questions, Mrs. Bobbsey began pulling away the logs, Nan lending her strength as best she could.

Flossie and Freddie, too, rushed in and tried to pull away the lighter poles and sticks, until their mother called to them:

"You two little ones keep away. You might pull out one that is keeping others and larger ones from falling on Bert. We must be careful."

After removing several of the larger tree trunks, Mrs. Bobbsey could look in amid the tangle of other timbers and see Bert penned there. The sticks were piled all about him in criss-cross fashion, and in this way the heavy weight was kept from crushing him.

Finally Mrs. Bobbsey took hold of one log so tightly wedged in by others that she could not move it. She and Nan tugged at it, but as they moved it a little it seemed as though the logs over Bert's head might crash down on him, and yet, with this log in place, it was hard to reach the others.

"We must be careful!" exclaimed Mrs. Bobbsey. "We need help, Nan. You had better go to the nearest house and get some of the men."

But at that moment the crash and crackle of breaking underbrush was heard, showing that someone was coming. For a moment Nan thought it might be her father approaching, and Mrs. Bobbsey half feared it might be some of the ugly lumbermen. But even they would have been welcome now.

However, the newcomer turned out to be a boy, rather older than Bert, a tall, strong-looking country chap. He saw at once that something was wrong.

"What's the matter?" he asked.

"My son, Bert, is pinned under that pile of logs," answered his mother.

"He tried to make a bear trap," explained Nan.

"Not much use making bear traps around here. No bears ever come to these parts," returned the farmer-boy. "But I'll help get him out."

He was strong and skilful and knew so much about moving the criss-crossed timbers and did it in such a clever way that in a little while, Nan and Mrs. Bobbsey helping, Bert was able to crawl out, not much the worse for his perilous adventure.

Bert was covered with dirt and bits of bark, and he limped a little where one log had pinched his right foot, but no bones were broken, and really he had come out of it very luckily.

"Don't build any more bear traps!" warned Bert's mother, when, with a sigh of relief, she saw that he was all right.

"I—I guess I won't," he promised.

"And we never can thank you enough," Mrs.

Bobbsey went on to the farmer-boy who had arrived just in time. "Do you live around here?"

"Yes, about two miles off. My name is Stoddard—William Stoddard. My father runs a farm."

"I think I have heard Mr. Bobbsey speak of your father," said the children's mother. "He said we might buy supplies there. We are camping out in a bungalow near some lumber Mr. Bobbsey has bought," she went on to explain.

"Yes, I heard there was a party camping here," said William, or "Bill," as he said he was more often called. "Well, I hope you have a nice time. It's fine weather now. And don't get into any more traps," he added to Bert, with a laugh.

"I won't!" agreed Nan's brother.

"Come and see us some time," urged Mrs. Bobbsey, as Bill walked on.

He promised to do so, and with a wave of his hand to Flossie and Freddie, who watched him with big eyes, he disappeared along the forest path.

"It's a good thing he happened to come," observed Bert, as he looked at the pile of twisted logs that had been his trap.

"Indeed it is," said Mrs. Bobbsey. "You gave us a fright. Don't try any more tricks, Bert."

When Mr. Bobbsey came home, after arranging to hire some men to help him move the logs, he agreed that Bert had had a very narrow escape.

"I must call and thank this Bill Stoddard," said Mr. Bobbsey.

"When can you get your timber into the lake?"

asked Mrs. Bobbsey that night after supper, when the doings of the day were being talked about.

"The men will be here in two or three days," was the answer.

"Oh, shall we have to go home then?" asked Nan.

"No," answered her father, "I shall have to stay here until the last log is floated away. I cannot take any chances of those men stealing my timber; though I don't believe they will try anything like that. Oh, you children will have plenty of fun camping out here, I can promise you that."

Nan and Bert went off the next day to explore the woods, while Mrs. Bobbsey and the smaller twins rowed about in a boat on the little cove in front of the bungalow. Mr. Bobbsey was busy making plans for fastening his logs into rafts to be floated down the lake as soon as his men should arrive.

Nan, seeing a bunch of red wild flowers that were strange to her at some distance from the path, ran on ahead of Bert to look at them closely.

As she leaned over to examine the flowers, the girl caught sight of something down in the grass. It was something coiled and spotted, and as Nan looked she saw this "something" open a mouth and from the mouth a black and forked tongue darted rapidly.

"Oh, Bert! Bert!"screamed Nan. "Here's a snake, and it's trying to bite me! Oh, Bert!"

Bert caught up a stick and sprang to aid his sister.

"Where is it? Where's the snake?" he cried.

"There," answered Nan, pointing. "Oh, it is trying to bite me!"

Bert saw the coiled reptile, but instead of striking at it, as Nan expected him to do, her brother laughed and dropped his club.

"Why don't you kill it?" asked Nan.

"What's the use?" asked Bert. "That's a harmless snake. It isn't poisonous and it's more scared than you are."

"Well, I'm scared enough!" declared Nan, as she moved away. "But what makes you say that snake isn't dangerous when he tried to bite me—or sting me with his tongue?"

"A snake doesn't sting with its tongue," declared Bert. "When snakes bite they do it with their teeth. And I suppose this snake has teeth, only they're small ones. But he wouldn't bite you, anyhow. He wants to get away. There he goes!"

As Bert pointed, Nan saw the reptile quickly wiggling away in the bushes, and it seemed glad to go.

"How do you know that snake wasn't poisonous?" asked Nan.

"Our teacher told us all about snakes," Bert answered. "In the United States there are only a few poisonous snakes, and none of them is around here. Rattlers and copperheads are the worst, but none has ever been seen here. And snakes that aren't poisonous do more good than harm."

"How?" asked Nan, who was getting interested.

"The snakes catch rats and mice that would eat the farmers' grain," explained Bert. "Farmers ought to be told not to kill snakes that aren't poisonous."

"I thought all snakes were poisonous," said Nan. "And I thought that they wanted to bite you when they ran their tongue in and out that way."

"That's silly!" declared Bert. "No snake stings, or bites, with its tongue, even though it is sharp and forked. Of course poisonous snakes are dangerous and ought to be killed, but not any snakes around here."

"Well, I'm glad to know that," said Nan, and she went on to examine the flowers, feeling that Bert was quite a smart and good brother. She had been taught not to pick wild flowers, which were being too quickly destroyed, but she took one blossom and a leaf so she could look it up in her flower book and find out what it was.

It was a few days after this that the Bobbsey twins went on a camping-out picnic for the day, tramping through the woods to a point farther up the shore of Lake Melrose.

"We may as well have a good time in the woods while I am waiting for my lumbermen to come and float the logs," said Mr. Bobbsey.

So baskets were packed with lunch, and, locking up the bungalow, the family started off. It was a lovely day and the woods were pleasant, the birds singing in the trees.

"It's just as nice as on Uncle Daniel's farm at Meadow Brook," said Nan, as she walked along beside Bert.

"Yes, but I wish Harry and Bob Guess were here to play with us," sighed Bert. "We could have a lot of fun."

"You mustn't call him Bob Guess any more," objected Nan. "His name is Bobbsey, like ours, since Uncle Dan adopted him."

"That's right—I forgot," admitted Bert.

It was fun, tramping through the woods, and it made them all hungry, so the children, especially, were quite ready to stop at noon and see what the lunch baskets contained. A large rug from the car had been brought along, and this was spread on the ground. Mrs. Bobbsey and Nan set out the good things, while Bert and his father made a fire.

"And here are two special little pies, one for Flossie and one for Freddie," said Mrs. Bobbsey, lifting them from a basket. "I made them of huckleberries, and I hope you'll like them."

"Oh, thank you! I love pie!" cried Freddie, and he put his little one on the ground beside him.

"So do I!" added Flossie. The pies were baked in saucers, and were just about the right size for small children.

When lunch was almost ready and they were

seated about the car rug spread on the ground Flossie suddenly caused a commotion by crying:

"Where's my pie? Where's my huckleberry pie? Somebody took it! Oh, maybe a bear came and took my huckleberry pie!"

CHAPTER VIII

THE BIG WIND

MRS. BOBBSEY, who had been about to pass some sandwiches to her husband, paused with the plate half-way across the rug that served as a table cloth and looked around.

"What's that, Flossie?" asked the little girl's mother. "Someone has taken your huckleberry pie, you say?"

"Yes. And maybe it was a bear," complained Flossie.

"Nonsense!" laughed Mr. Bobbsey. "If ever there were any bears around here they ran away after they heard Bert was building a trap to catch them," and Mr. Bobbsey looked at his son with a twinkle in his eye.

"Well, somebody took my pie!" said Flossie, almost ready to cry.

"It isn't around here," announced Nan, looking about. "And I saw it in front of Flossie a moment ago."

"Did either of you boys take Flossie's pie to tease her?" asked Mrs. Bobbsey, looking first at Bert and then at Freddie.

"I didn't," said Bert.

"And I have a huckleberry pie of my own," announced Freddie. "I'll give Flossie some of my pie if a bear took hers," he added kindly.

"There are no bears!" exclaimed Mr. Bobbsey.

"Oh, I see where the pie is!" cried Nan.

"Where?" they all asked.

"Flossie is sitting on it!" laughed Nan. "Look! She's sitting right on it!"

And there, sure enough, under Flossie's fat, chubby legs could be seen the edge of the little huckleberry pie in the saucer.

"Oh, Flossie!" cried Mrs. Bobbsey. "Your clothes will be all stained!"

"And I guess the pie will be spoiled," chuckled Mr. Bobbsey. "Never mind, that's a small accident to happen on a picnic. We'll have a good time even if Flossie did sit on her pie."

"Oh, dear!" murmured the little golden-haired girl, as she stood up and looked down at the pie.

But it was not as much harmed as had been feared, and, luckily, not much juice had been crushed out on Flossie's clothes. So, after all, the damage was small and the pie was still good enough to eat.

"I'm glad a bear didn't take my pie," said Flossie, as she ate her pastry.

After the picnic lunch the Bobbseys walked farther up along Lake Melrose, to a place where they had never before been. It was wild and beautiful in the woods.

Not all the lunch had been eaten, for Mrs. Bobbsey had packed the baskets full, and she knew, from past experience, that the children would be hungry again in the afternoon before they got back to the bungalow.

"Oh, what a lovely place for a swing!" cried Nan, as they reached a little glade and saw one large tree with a big branch stretching out—just right for a swing rope.

"But we haven't any rope," said Mrs. Bobbsey.

"Maybe we could make one out of a wild grape vine," suggested Bert. "Some of us fellows did that in the woods once, and we had a fine swing."

"Is it strong enough?" asked Nan.

"Plenty," declared Bert. "Here, I'll show you how to make a swing from a grape vine."

Many vines were growing on the edge of the glade, and with his father's help Bert fastened two ends of a long vine to the overhanging branch, letting the loop trail down.

"We haven't any swing board, but you can sit on the vine," said Bert, and Nan did this while her brother pushed her. The swing worked very well, too, and Flossie and Freddie took turns in it.

"Don't you want to try, Mother?" asked Nan, as she saw her parents sitting on the mossy ground beneath a tree, talking.

"Thank you, but I'm afraid I'm too heavy for the grape vine," replied Mrs. Bobbsey.

And, as she was rather plump, probably it is just

as well that she did not sit on the swing. But the children had lots of fun. Bert and Nan tired of the game before Flossie and Freddie did, and the older twins let the smaller ones have the vine, while Bert led his sister deeper into the woods.

"Where are we going?" asked Nan.

"I want to go up on top of a hill I saw, and maybe we can get a look at the lake from there," explained Bert. For they had, by this time, walked so far into the woods on their picnic tramp that they had lost sight of Lake Melrose.

"I hope there aren't any snakes here," remarked Nan, as she followed her brother along a small path.

"They won't hurt you if they are here. They'll run away if you give them the chance," Bert reminded her.

"Well, I'd just as soon not see them," said Nan.

After a hard climb Bert and his sister reached the top of a hill, from which they had a glimpse of Lake Melrose. It was a beautiful sheet of water, fully as pretty as their own Lake Metoka.

"But look at those black clouds over there!" exclaimed Nan, pointing to the western edge of the lake, where, indeed, the sky was covered with dense, black masses of clouds. "It looks as if a storm might be coming."

"You're right, it does!" agreed Bert. "Guess we'd better run back and tell the others. They can't see it from down in the woods where they are."

When Nan and Bert got back to where Flossie and Freddie were still swinging and where Mr. and Mrs.

Bobbsey were talking under the tree, the older twins exclaimed:

"We'd better be going! A storm is coming!"

"Are you sure?" asked Mr. Bobbsey. And when Bert and Nan had told him what they had seen he agreed with them.

"I was going to give the children some more lunch," said Mrs. Bobbsey as she arose. "They must be hungry, and it is a long way back home. Perhaps we shouldn't have come so far."

"Oh, we'll get back all right," declared Mr. Bobbsey. "As for lunch, I think, as long as we may get a storm, that it would be better to start back now and eat later."

"Do you think it will thunder?" asked Freddie, pressing close to his mother.

"An' lighten?" added Flossie. The small twins did not like big storms, especially of the thunder and lightning kind.

"Oh, I don't believe it will thunder very hard," said Mrs. Bobbsey. "Don't be afraid. Now help gather up the things and we'll go home."

Quick preparations were made for leaving, but fast as the Bobbseys acted, the storm was quicker. On account of the thick trees they could not see it gathering force as it swept across the lake. And the first real warning they had, except for that given by Nan and Bert, was when the trees above them were suddenly swept by a heavy gust of wind, so that the branches swayed and creaked alarmingly.

"It's going to blow hard!" cried Mr. Bobbsey.

"Come on, children! Nan, you look after Flossie. Bert, you take Freddie!"

Before they could advance more than a dozen steps the wind was blowing so very hard that it was all they could do to walk along. All about them the gale howled, small branches were broken off the trees and the Bobbseys were pelted under a shower of leaves. It was like a hurricane.

"There goes my hat!" cried Freddie, as the wind carried it from his head.

"And there goes the car rug!" added Mrs. Bobbsey, as the gale whipped it from her arm, over which she had placed it. "This is a terrible storm! What had we better do, Dick?"

Mr. Bobbsey looked up and caught sight of the sky covered with inky-black clouds, while the wind blew harder and harder.

CHAPTER IX

A STORMY NIGHT

BERT BOBBSEY, with a yell that was filled as much with delight at the big wind as with fear, raced after the car rug which the wind had carried from his mother's arm.

"Hi!" shouted Bert. "This is fun! Watch me tackle that rug! I'm a football player!"

And Bert gave rather a good imitation of a player on the field. He caught the rug as the wind whipped it about a bush, and then Bert wound the blanket around him.

"Now I'm an Indian!" he shouted. "Look at me dance!"

But in spite of the fun Bert was having, Mr. and Mrs. Bobbsey were really worried about the children being out in the storm. Flossie and Freddie clung together, and Nan, after having first laughed at Bert's funny capers, anxiously watched first the gathering storm and then her father and mother.

"We must hurry back to our camp," said Mr. Bobbsey, as he took his wife's arm to guide her through the forest.

"Perhaps there won't be any camp left when we get there," she said, in a low voice.

"What do you mean?" asked Mr. Bobbsey quickly.

"That bungalow is very old and shaky," his wife replied. "It wouldn't take much of a blow to send it into the lake."

"Oh, nonsense!" laughed Mr. Bobbsey. "It will be all right."

"Let us hope so."

"Do you think your logs will blow into the lake?" asked Nan, who had heard only a few words of the talk between her father and mother.

"No. But if they should it would save the men the work of rolling them into the water," said Mr. Bobbsey. "But come along now. Have we everything?" he asked, as he looked over the place where they had eaten their lunch.

"I think so," answered his wife. "Gracious, how it blows!" she cried, as she staggered on, carrying a box and a basket which contained the remains of the food. Nan and Mr. Bobbsey carried the rest of the picnic things, while Bert had all he could manage to keep the rug from blowing away again, and Flossie and Freddie, hand in hand, walked near their older brother and sister.

It was, indeed, a fierce wind storm. As the Bobbseys slowly made their way through the forest, they saw here and there amid the trees glimpses of the lake. Its waters were being whipped into white-capped waves by the wind.

"I'm glad we're not out on the lake," observed Mrs. Bobbsey.

"It would be great to have a sailboat there!" cried Bert.

"You wouldn't have it very long," said his father. "The wind would tear the sail to pieces."

"Look!" cried Flossie. "The wind is blowing all the leaves off the trees. There won't be any left!" And indeed it did seem as though the gale would strip all the green from the forest trees as they leaned far over in the terrific gale. The air was filled with flying bits of green, some of which struck the faces of the Bobbseys and made the flesh smart.

"Well, I'm glad there's no lightning," observed Freddie.

"And thunder," said Flossie. "I hate thunder!"

So far the big wind seemed to be the only part of the gathering storm, but even as Flossie and her brother spoke of the thunder and lightning, there sounded off in the west a low rumble and roar.

"Is that—is that thunder?" faltered Freddie.

"Oh, yes, just a little thunder," answered his mother, who wanted to tell Freddie the truth, yet not frighten him.

"An' it's awful sharp lightning," sighed Flossie, clinging closer to her mother, as a bright flash blazed up in the dark woods. "I wish we were home."

"It isn't sharp enough to cut you," laughed Bert. He and Nan were not afraid of thunder storms.

Louder grew the thunder and brighter the lightning. Here and there branches, broken from the trees, crashed down on either side of the Bobbseys or in front or behind them, but no one was hit. Mrs. Bobbsey looked at her husband once or twice, as if to ask him whether or not it was wise to keep on going through the storm. But he nodded his head "yes", and on they went.

"We must get back to the bungalow if we can," Mr. Bobbsey said to his wife. "This storm is going to get worse instead of passing away, and it will soon be night."

"Are we far from the cabin?" asked Mrs. Bobbsey.

"Farther than I wish we were," said Mr. Bobbsey. "It's a long way back to our camp. We shouldn't have come so far, but I had no idea a storm was coming. Goodness, the lake is rough!"

He said this as he looked through the trees and caught sight of the tumbling white-capped waves of Lake Melrose. In one place the path led close to the edge of the water and the waves could be heard beating on the small sandy beach.

"It's almost like Ocean Cliff, where Uncle William lives at Sunset Beach," called Nan to Bert.

"The sea is rougher than the lake," observed Bert.

"Well, the lake is bad enough," said Nan, as they turned again into the deeper part of the woods and could no longer see the tumbling water.

At last Mr. Bobbsey came to a stop in a little glen, where a pile of rocks and fallen trees formed a sort of cave.

"I think we had better stay here for a while," he said to his wife. "It's going to pour bucketfuls in a few minutes and we'll be drenched if we're out in it. Here we can make a sort of shelter with the car rug —for the children at least."

"I don't mind getting wet!" exclaimed Bert, who had managed to keep hold of the rug, though at times the wind almost tore it from his hands.

"I don't want any of us to get wet if it can be helped," remarked Mr. Bobbsey. "So, Bert, you and I will make a shelter. You, too, Nan, help me get some of those tree branches and we'll lay them across these rocks. That will make part of a roof, and we can spread the car rug over the branches for better protection."

"That rug isn't waterproof," said Mrs. Bobbsey.

"No," agreed her husband. "But it will keep out most of the water. And it's going to rain very soon."

Bert and Nan and their father worked fast. Mrs. Bobbsey started to help, but she had all she could do to comfort Freddie and Flossie who grew more and more afraid as the thunder boomed louder and the lightning flashed more brightly. However, Mrs. Bobbsey thought of a way to take the minds of the smaller twins off their main trouble.

"See!" she said. "We're going to stay in a real rocky den."

"Like a bear?" asked Freddie. "Oh, that will be fun! We'll pretend we're bears, Flossie!"

"Maybe there's bears in that den already," said Flossie. And this made a new cause for fear until

Mrs. Bobbsey, with a laugh, went in the den and came out again laughing as she told them:

"No bears in there, and it's nice and dry. Come on."

"I think it will be a fine place to stay when there's a roof on," observed Nan. "We'll play house, Flossie and Freddie," she added. "We'll have fun."

This idea pleased the smaller twins so they laughed instead of looking fearfully around every time it lightened or thundered. Mr. Bobbsey and the older twins worked hard, and soon had the gap in the rocks roofed over with tree branches. On these leaves and sticks were piled, and over all the car rug was spread, though this was not easy, as the wind blew it about.

But at last the rug was in place, and then on top of that some rocks and heavy branches were piled so that a fairly good roof was in place. And just in time, too, for as the Bobbseys crowded back into the rocky cave, or "den", as Flossie and Freddie called it, the rain pelted down.

"My, what a storm!" exclaimed Nan, as she heard the howl of the wind, the boom of the thunder and the rattle of the rain on the leaves.

"But we are lucky to have such a good shelter," said Mrs. Bobbsey cheerfully.

"Oh, yes, it's going to be fun!" was Nan's quick reply. "And we'll play house, for we have something to eat."

Luckily nearly half the picnic lunch was left in the baskets and boxes, and as soon as the smaller twins heard the word "eat", they imagined themselves hungry again; and they may have been, for it was some time since they had had dinner.

"It's a good thing the wind blows away from us, instead of into this cave," said Mr. Bobbsey. "Otherwise the wind would send the rain all over us, even if we have a roof on. As long as the wind holds this way we'll be all right."

"Can't you make a fire and have it light?" asked Flossie. "It's getting dark, Daddy."

Night, indeed, was setting in, but it would have been dark without that, as the sky was covered with lowering rain clouds.

"I'm afraid all the electricity is in the sky," laughed Mrs. Bobbsey. "And there isn't any gas, nor have we a lantern. We'll have to stay in the dark, I guess. But then no mosquitoes can find us," she added, for this is what she used to tell the small twins at home when, occasionally, they begged for a light in their bedroom.

However, Bert unexpectedly cried out:

"I have a torch!"

"Have you?" asked his father. "That's good. Let me have it and I'll see if we can't make a sort of bed back here in the cave."

It was much darker far back in the little den than it was outside, though soon it would be black night all over. Taking Bert's torch, and thinking to himself how lucky it was the boy had brought it, Mr. Bobbsey went into the far end of the den. He gave a joyful cry.

"There are a lot of fine dry leaves here," he said. "You children can burrow down in them just as the bears do when they take their long, winter sleep. Oh, this is going to be a fine place!"

The torch was a small but very bright one, though of course it would not burn long if left turned on. Mr. Bobbsey flashed it long enough for them all to see the pile of dry leaves far back in the rocky den, and then, putting it out, he went near the entrance to the den.

"We'd better eat out here where we can see a little without the torch," he said. "We'll need that when it gets very dark—in the middle of the night maybe."

"Oh, shall we have to stay here all night?" asked Nan, greatly excited.

"Yes, I think so," her father answered. "It would never do to try to go through the woods in this storm. A tree might fall on us. Here we are safe and dry, though it isn't as good a place to sleep in as our bungalow at the camp. But we must do the best we can."

Louder rumbled the thunder and brighter the lightning, while the rain came down, as Mr. Bobbsey said, in "bucketfuls". As the stormy night settled down the Bobbseys huddled together in the cave, while the drops pelted down on the roof.

"I don't like it here! I don't like it!" sobbed Freddie.

"Neither do I! I want to go home!" wailed Flossie.

CHAPTER X

LOST

THE smaller Bobbsey twins were just on the verge of tears. They might start crying any moment. But Mrs. Bobbsey and Nan, at the same moment, thought of a way to stop this.

"We're going to have something to eat right away," said Mrs. Bobbsey cheerfully. "Bert, you open the baskets and boxes, please, and here's a flat rock like a little table."

This caused a smile to appear on the faces of Freddie and Flossie. Then Nan said:

"Don't you little twins dare cry in here! You'll get the cave all wet, and goodness knows it's wet enough outside! Keep it dry in here! Don't cry!"

This made Flossie and Freddie not only smile, but laugh, and so their fears and discontent were driven away. And when Bert and Nan spread out the food—well, it was quite a happy little party.

Some big stones were found for seats, being rolled to the flat rock that served as a table. Though the storm kept up and it grew darker and darker, except when a lightning flash sprang from cloud to cloud, it was still bright enough in the front part of the cave to see to eat. Sandwiches and pieces of cake were passed about, and there was part of a bottle of lemonade which the children drank.

Mrs. Bobbsey would have liked a cup of hot tea, she said later, but it would not have been wise to make a fire in the leaf-filled den, even if a blaze could have been started without having the wind blow it out. For the wind blew round the den in great gusts as the storm swept through the woods.

"Please, could I have just a teeny bit more cake?" asked Flossie.

"Here you are!" laughed Nan. "Will you have chocolate, sponge or angel cake?" she asked.

"There's only one kind!" declared Freddie.

"I know there is. I was only joking," and Nan laughed again. "Here, Flossie," she went on, passing something to her little sister. Flossie put it in her mouth, but at once cried out:

"That isn't cake! It's a piece of bread and butter!"

"Oh, is it?" asked Nan. "Well, it's so dark I can hardly see."

"I'll turn on the torch for a moment," offered Mr. Bobbsey, "though I want to save it as much as I can."

Under the gleam of the light that Bert had so luckily brought in his pocket, a piece of cake was picked out for Flossie.

The smaller twins were getting tired and sleepy,

even though the noise of the storm could plainly be heard outside their den.

"I'll put you to bed in the leaves, like the Babes in the Wood, Flossie and Freddie," said Mrs. Bobbsey. "Come on. It's a queer bed for you, but I think it will be lots of fun, and you can snuggle down like the little bears and keep warm."

"We'll just have to stay here," said Mr. Bobbsey, as he looked out into the darkness that now surrounded the mouth of the cave. "It would be impossible to find our bungalow in this storm, especially after dark. We're lucky to have found this shelter."

"And the roof doesn't leak very much," added Bert.

"Even if it does, later on, we can get far enough back under the overhanging rock to keep sheltered," said his father. "The worst of the storm is over, but it sounds as if it would rain all night."

The thunder and lightning had stopped, but the rain was still pelting down, and, as Mr. Bobbsey said, looked like keeping on for some time.

However, the family was used to roughing it and they had been camping before, so they did not mind a little discomfort. A little of the food remained for breakfast, though Mrs. Bobbsey could not help sighing as she thought how Flossie and Freddie would call in vain for their hot porridge with cream and sugar.

"But when morning comes we'll soon be back at our camp," she said to her husband.

"I hope so," he answered.

The torch was used long enough to make "nests" in the pile of dried leaves for Flossie and Freddie. They said their prayers, cuddled down together with all their clothes on, and were soon sound asleep. Luckily it was not cold in the cave.

Bert and Nan sat up a little longer with their father and mother. They sat in the darkness, listening to the pelting of the rain and talking of their day's adventures. At last Bert and Nan grew tired and sleepy, and Mrs. Bobbsey suggested that they lie down, one on either side of Flossie and Freddie, and get a little rest.

"I know I shan't sleep a wink!" declared Nan.

"Couldn't I stay up with you, Dad?" Bert pleaded, blinking his eyes to keep them open.

"What would be the use?" asked Mr. Bobbsey. "There is no need to keep watch."

"Something might happen. Something might come in during the night," suggested Bert.

"Oh, nonsense!" laughed his father. "Go to bed, Bert."

Then Bert crawled in the leaves. In spite of Nan saying she would not "sleep a wink", her eyes closed almost at once and she was in dreamland. Bert, too, very soon dropped off to sleep.

Mr. and Mrs. Bobbsey sat down on a pile of leaves with their backs against the stone wall of the den. They were too anxious to go easily to sleep. Besides, though he said nothing to Bert about it, Mr. Bobbsey intended to remain awake all night.

"My, how it rains!" said Mrs. Bobbsey, as an hour or two passed in darkness and the water still pelted from the sky.

"Yes, it is a hard storm," agreed her husband.

"Do you think anything may happen back at the bungalow?" asked his wife.

"Well, the wind blew pretty hard and the bungalow was none too strong—it's only an old shack," he replied.

"I'm almost glad we're not in it now," said the mother of the now sleeping twins. "But do you imagine those men may come and take your timber in this storm?" she went on.

"I hardly believe so," Mr. Bobbsey answered. "They'll be only too glad to stay in their own shelter on a night like this. I fancy my logs will be all right, and in another week I'll have them made up into rafts, floating down the lake. Then we'll go back home."

"The children seem to like it here, even if we are caught out in a storm," said Mrs. Bobbsey. Then she put her head against the side of the den and, like the children, fell asleep.

Mr. Bobbsey closed his eyes and dozed off in spite of the fact that he had made up his mind not to go to sleep.

Suddenly a loud crash sounded outside the cave, and the roof seemed to tremble.

"What's that?" cried Mrs. Bobbsey, starting up.

Another crash, louder than the first, sounded, and so close that Mr. Bobbsey leaped to his feet.

"Trees are falling outside the cave," he said. "The rain has washed the dirt away from the roots, and the wind has blown them over. One must have fallen near us and some branches landed on the roof. We had better get back under the edge of the rock where the children are. Then we'll be safe."

This they did, another tree falling outside the cave as they changed their places. But, luckily, the heavy rocks protected the Bobbseys.

Morning came, and the sun shining into the cave dazzled Mr. Bobbsey's eyes and awakened him.

"My goodness, but I'm lame and stiff!" he cried, as he stood up and stamped his feet, for one of his legs was "asleep", as it is called. Mrs. Bobbsey, also, could hardly move, but after stretching a bit she felt better, and so did her husband.

"The children seem all right," he said, for the twins were still sleeping.

"Yes, it wasn't such a bad night for them," said Mrs. Bobbsey. "But, oh, for a cup of hot coffee!"

"We'll soon have that," laughed Mr. Bobbsey, brushing off the leaves that clung to him.

Bert and Nan and Flossie and Freddie were soon awakened, and for a moment or two they could not remember where they were. Then they laughed and said it seemed hardly any time at all since they had crawled into the leaves the night before. They had slept soundly and warmly, and had not heard the crash of falling trees.

When they went to leave the cave to get out into the warm sunshine, it was found that one of the trees had fallen across the mouth of the den in such a way that there was hardly room to crawl out. However, after Mr. Bobbsey had broken off some of the branches a hole was made so Mrs. Bobbsey and the others could wriggle their way out.

"Oh, it's good to be in the sunshine again!" cried Mrs. Bobbsey, as she shook out her crumpled skirt. "And now for home!" she added. "Home and breakfast!"

"Haven't we got anything to eat left?" asked Flossie.

"There isn't very much," said her mother. "You may have what there is."

Dried sandwiches and bits of cake did not make a very good breakfast, but Flossie and Freddie, at least, seemed to enjoy it, and ate all that was given them down to the last crumb.

Then, having drunk some water from a spring and having washed their faces and hands, the campers of the night were ready to start on their homeward trip.

The wind had gone down, the rain had ceased, and the woods were bathed in warm sunshine. Except for fallen trees and many broken branches, with more than the usual amount of leaves scattered on the ground, no one would have known there had been such a storm.

"I hope we find everything all right at the bungalow," thought Mr. Bobbsey to himself, though he said nothing to the rest about any worries he might have.

"I'm going fishing when I get back," announced

Freddie, as they all trudged through the forest. "Fish like to be caught after a big storm."

"I didn't think fish ever liked to be caught," observed Nan. "That is, not by the way they wiggle on the hook."

"Oh, fish like to be caught, and I'm going to catch some," declared Freddie. "Then we'll have 'em for breakfast."

"I'm afraid we won't have time to wait for breakfast until you catch fish," laughed his mother. "Luckily I have some things in the bungalow pantry."

They started out from the cave, and tramped on for a mile.

"There's the lake," said Mr. Bobbsey, after a while. "Now we'll follow that and soon be home."

He pointed to where water could be seen gleaming in the sunshine amid the trees. Flossie and Freddie ran on ahead, Bert and Nan coming next, and Mr. and Mrs. Bobbsey bringing up the rear of the procession.

The small twins began to cast stones into the water as they reached it, but when Bert and Nan arrived at the edge and looked across to the other shore, Bert cried out:

"This isn't Lake Melrose!"

"It isn't?" asked his father.

"No," said Bert. "This is only a small pond or lake. It isn't Melrose at all!"

"That's true," admitted Mr. Bobbsey, as he came out of the woods and looked across the rippling water. "We've come the wrong way. It isn't our lake at all."

"Are we lost?" asked Nan.

"I'm afraid we are—a little," admitted her father. "But we'll soon find ourselves," he added, with a smile. "We just came the wrong way. All we need to do is to turn around and go back. We'll soon be at home."

CHAPTER XI

A BROKEN BUNGALOW

IT was easy to say, "We'll soon be at home." But Mr. Bobbsey was a stranger in the woods around Lake Melrose, never having been more than half a mile from the place where his timber was stacked, and, going on their picnic, the Bobbseys had travelled several miles from their camp.

Mr. Bobbsey thought it would be easy enough to go back to the place where they had spent the night, in the rocky den, and from there reach Lake Melrose.

"Once I'm on the shore of the lake it will be easy enough to follow the beach and get back to the bungalow," he said.

"That is, if you don't go the wrong way and walk away from our camp instead of towards it," said Mrs. Bobbsey.

"Oh, I shan't do that," declared her husband.

"But that's what we did to get to this pond, instead of to our own lake this morning," said Bert.

"Yes, I did start off the wrong way," admitted Mr. Bobbsey. "I should have gone east, and, instead, I came west. But we'll soon get back to where the cave is, and after that it will be easy."

But it was not, and after walking for some time, Flossie and Freddie lagging behind a little, Mrs. Bobbsey said:

"I don't believe, Dick, that we are going right at all!"

"We don't seem to be," agreed her husband. "We should have been at the cave long before this. The woods are so thick I can't get a good look at the sun to tell which way we ought to walk. I should have brought a compass."

"Can't you look at the trees and tell the north side 'cause that has most moss on?" asked Bert.

"That isn't always a safe guide," replied his father. "But don't worry. We'll soon get on the path, and though we may be a little late for breakfast, we'll get there sooner or later."

"I want my breakfast now!" demanded Flossie.

"I'm hungry, too," said Freddie.

"There isn't anything left," sighed Mrs. Bobbsey. "It's too bad, but——"

"Hark!" suddenly called Nan. "I think I hear someone coming!"

They all listened and plainly heard the crackle of underbrush and small tree branches as a heavy foot was set on them. Who or what could it be?

"Maybe—maybe it's a bear?" whispered Flossie to Freddie.

"No bears in these woods!" laughed Bert, as he caught the frightened tone of his little sister.

"It's a man," declared Mr. Bobbsey. "I can tell by his walk."

Then a new thought came to Nan and Bert. Perhaps it was one of the ugly lumbermen who wanted to make trouble for their father.

"Hello! Hello!" called Mr. Bobbsey.

"Hello!" came back the answer. "Who are you? What's the matter?"

"We're lost, I guess. Can you put us on the trail to Lake Melrose? We want to get back to Kling's lumber camp where we have a bungalow."

The other did not answer, but the tramping in the underbrush grew louder and then there came into view a tall farm lad at the sight of whom the Bobbseys shouted with joy.

"It's Bill Stoddard!" exclaimed Bert.

"Oh, hello! I didn't know it was you," said Bill, with a smile on his good-natured face. "So you're lost, are you?"

"Yes," admitted Mr. Bobbsey. "I didn't know your place was so near here, or I wouldn't have felt worried."

"Our house isn't so near here as you think," said Bill. "I'm out in the woods hunting a lost cow. That's what brings me here. But I guess I'll have to give up and go back. I can take you to our place. It's about two miles. But what brings you out so early? You must have had a quick breakfast."

"We haven't had any—not a bit!" quickly said

Nan. "That is," she added, "not enough. Just a little dried-out food left from yesterday's lunch."

"Oh, that's too bad!" exclaimed the farm boy. "Well, I had a bite before I started out after this cow that got lost in the storm last night, and I'm going back now and fill up on some more. Won't you come with me? Mother will be glad to give you breakfast."

"Oh, how wonderful!" cried Mrs. Bobbsey. "You see we've been out all night," she added.

"Like your cow," said Bert, with a smile at Bill.

"Out all night!" exclaimed Bill. "All of you; the whole family?"

Then they quickly told him the story, and of how they had stayed in the cave all night and had become lost trying to find the way back to their bungalow.

"That's too bad!" exclaimed the Stoddard lad. "Well, your troubles will soon be over. I wish mine were—I mean I wish I could find that lost cow. You didn't see her, did you?" he asked the wanderers.

"No," said Bert. "But I'll help you look for her after breakfast."

"An' I want my breakfast now!" demanded Flossie.

"Come on, I'll give you a pick-a-back!" offered Bill to the little girl.

"And I'll carry Freddie," chimed in Bert. "We'll get breakfast quicker if we take them that way."

This was true, for the small twins could not walk as fast as the older ones in the party. Perched on the boys' backs, Flossie and Freddie had comfortable rides and it was jolly good fun for the small twins.

They laughed and shouted as Bert and Bill pretended to be skittish horses and pranced around. Mr. and Mrs. Bobbsey smiled at the fun the children were having.

Through the woods, along a path Bill Stoddard knew well, the farmer boy led his friends until at last they came out on top of a grassy hill.

"There's our house!" cried Bill, pointing to the farm down below.

"Really, I never was so glad to see a place before in all my life!" cried Mrs. Bobbsey. "I can almost smell the coffee!"

"I guess Mother will just about have the regular breakfast ready," observed Bill. "Sometimes, when there are things to do early, we get a bite to eat and come back to a regular breakfast later. That's what I'm doing now."

Down the hill they went, turning into a lane and then along a road that led to the comfortable-looking farmhouse. Bert and Nan sniffed the air. There was no doubt of it—coffee was being brewed in the warm and cosy kitchen.

"Hello, Bill! Is that you?" called a woman's voice, as the party neared the house. "Did you find the cow?"

"No, but I found a starving family!" Bill answered.

"Land sakes!" cried Mrs. Stoddard, as she opened the door, and then she laughed and welcomed the Bobbseys, who were soon seated about a table, eating their first real meal in several hours.

"It's lucky you found that cave to stay in," said

Mr. Stoddard, as he came in to hear the story. "That was a bad storm last night."

"And we slept in leaves like bear cubs!" laughed Flossie.

"And I wasn't afraid—not very much," added Freddie, while the others laughed.

After breakfast Mr. Stoddard said Bill could hitch up a horse and drive the Bobbseys back to their camp, as the distance was rather too far for the small twins to walk—or be carried pick-a-back.

"Then if we're going back in the wagon," said Mrs. Bobbsey, "I might as well buy some supplies from you, Mrs. Stoddard, if I may. I was coming over to ask about it towards the end of the week. I'll need eggs and other things."

A basket of food and supplies was purchased from the farmer's wife, and then the trip back was begun. On the way Bert and Bill kept their eyes open for a sight of the missing cow, though Bill said she might wander back by herself during the day.

"This is better than tramping around in the woods, lost and not knowing where to go," said Mrs. Bobbsey.

"Yes," agreed her husband, as Bill drove them along. "But I shan't get lost again. I'll always take a compass with me after this."

They were soon on the road that led around the lake shore, and in half an hour more were on familiar ground.

"This is our camping place. I know it," called Bert. "I can see your lumber pile, Dad!" he called.

"Yes, but where's our bungalow?" asked Nan. "It's gone! The bungalow is gone!"

"The bungalow gone! Impossible!" exclaimed Mrs. Bobbsey.

Mr. Bobbsey gave a whistle of surprise.

"It isn't exactly gone," he said. "But it's all broken up. It must have blown down in the storm last night. I was afraid of this!"

As the horse came to a stop they all looked at the place where the bungalow had stood. Now the house was only a ruin—a pile of twisted and tangled logs!

CHAPTER XII

CAMPING OUT

"HOW did that happen?"

"Was there a fire?"

These and other questions the Bobbsey twins fired at their father and mother as they stood looking at the ruins of what had been their bungalow.

"There wasn't any fire," said Mr. Bobbsey, for there was no trace of blackened logs nor smoke and there were no black embers as there would have been after a fire. "The wind must have blown it down. Well, it's too bad, but I'm glad it happened when we were out of it. The rocky den was a safer place last night than our bungalow would have been."

"Do you suppose those lumbermen had anything to do with this, Dick?" asked Mrs. Bobbsey, in a low voice.

"No, I think not," he answered, while the four twins climbed over some of the piled-up logs, followed by Bill Stoddard. "The men would have had no object in destroying our bungalow. All they want, so they claim, is pay for their work, or else they want to take the logs. But I shall not pay them for I do not owe them any money, and I certainly shall not let them take my timber."

"I thought, at first, they might have chopped down the bungalow just to be mean and ugly," went on Mrs. Bobbsey.

"No, it was the wind," said her husband again. "It really was almost half down, anyhow. But I thought it would last what little time we are to be here. However, even a well-built camp might have been blown down in such a wind as we had last night. I'm glad our boats are safe."

"We must see if we can save anything out of the wreck," said Mrs. Bobbsey, with a sigh. "I'm glad we had breakfast at Mrs. Stoddard's, for we never could have prepared any here. And I'm glad I brought some things to eat back with us. For it doesn't look as though we could cook on that stove ever again," and Mrs. Bobbsey pointed to the one that could be seen amid the wreck of the logs. "I must see if I can get at some of the children's clothes, and yours and mine, Dick."

"Yes, we need our things," agreed Mr. Bobbsey.

"Is there anything I can do to help?" asked Bill.

"I don't know," replied Mr. Bobbsey slowly. "If you aren't in a hurry you might wait a few minutes. I don't know just what we are going to do yet. It's quite a surprise—coming back to find your house blown down."

"It's like the three little pigs, Grunter, Squeaky

and Twisty-Tail," laughed Flossie, who remembered that story.

Bidding the children keep out of danger, for they would have climbed all over the wreckage but for this, Mr. and Mrs. Bobbsey looked for the things they had left in the bungalow when they had started out on the picnic the day before.

"Why, a lot of things are gone!" exclaimed Mrs. Bobbsey, searching in a place where a cupboard had been.

"So they are," agreed her husband. "Some of my things, too! Some papers and books that I need."

"And some of your clothing, too," added Mrs. Bobbsey. "The wind couldn't have blown all the missing things away, Dick!"

"No, I think people have been here and helped themselves," admitted Mr. Bobbsey.

"Those lumbermen, do you think?" asked his wife.

"Perhaps," he admitted. "But don't tell the children."

"Oh, dear!" sighed Mrs. Bobbsey, "this is a great piece of bad luck. Be careful, Flossie!" she cried, as she saw the little girl venturing too near a dangerous pile of logs. "I think," went on Mrs. Bobbsey as the children gathered around her, "that we had better pack up what things we have left and go home. Our car is safe, at least," she said, for it was under a shed and had not suffered much from the storm, nor had anyone tried to take it. "Yes, we had better go back home," she continued.

"Oh, no! Let's stay!" cried the children.

"But we have no place to stay—no place to eat or sleep," replied Mrs. Bobbsey.

"You could stay at our house," suggested Bill. "We'd be glad to have you all."

"That is very kind of you," said Mrs. Bobbsey, with a smile. "But we could not think of troubling your mother. No, we came here unexpectedly, after having had one holiday. It will be school time shortly, and the children will do well enough at home."

"Oh, it won't be school for a long while!" cried Nan.

"And we can have lots of fun here!" added Bert. "We were just beginning to have fun."

"We like it here," said Freddie, and Flossie agreed with him.

"But where can we stay?" asked Mrs. Bobbsey, pointing to the ruins of the bungalow. "What home we had is blown down!"

"We could live in a tent," put in Mr. Bobbsey. "It wouldn't be the first time."

"A tent!" cried Mrs. Bobbsey. "But it would take so long to buy and bring a tent up here, set it up and fix it so we could live in it. No, we had better go back home. It won't be long before the holidays are over."

"If you really wouldn't mind camping out in a tent for a week or so, I can fix it," said Mr. Bobbsey. "For my part, I'd like to stay here and guard my logs until I can float them down the lake. But I don't want you and the children to stay if you don't like it," he ended.

"Oh, I like it here, and the children seem to love it," admitted Mrs. Bobbsey. "But a tent—I don't see—oh, it's all so upsetting!"

"Now don't worry," advised her husband, with a laugh. "As for the tent, it is already here—or so near that it will not take long to get it."

"Here? What do you mean?" asked his wife wonderingly.

"Well," he went on, "when we first talked of coming up here I wasn't sure what condition the bungalow would be in; so I had a tent sent up, with camp beds and all the necessary supplies. But when I found the bungalow was in fairly good shape, I decided it would be more comfortable to live in that. I left the tent at the railway goods office, with all the supplies, and it's there yet. It will take only half a day to send for it and have it set up. Shall I do it?"

"Oh, then we could camp out in real earnest!" cried Nan.

"We'd have jolly good times!" shouted Bert.

"I want to go fishing!" was all Freddie could think of to say.

The tent was news to Mrs. Bobbsey, and she was surprised. But, after thinking it over and seeing how disappointed the children would be if they were taken home now, she agreed to stay.

"Then, Bill, there is something you can do for us," said Mr. Bobbsey. "Drive me to the railway station and I'll get some men to bring the tent here and put it up. It will not take long. We can use the floor of the bungalow."

"Oh, isn't this going to be lovely!" cried Nan.

"This is going to be the best holiday we ever had!" decided Bert.

While Mr. Bobbsey and Bill drove to the station, the children helped their mother in saving what they could from the wreck of the bungalow. Of course Flossie and Freddie could not be expected to see that anything was missing, and though Bert and Nan noticed and spoke about several things they wanted, their mother did not tell them the things were gone. The older twins just imagined they might be under the pile of boards and logs.

But Mrs. Bobbsey was sure that many things had been stolen, and among these things were a number of tins of food. Luckily they had plenty left, and they could get more at the farm.

It was noon when Bill and Mr. Bobbsey came back with some camp things on the wagon. The tent would be brought up in a big delivery van before night, Mr. Bobbsey said, and men would come to set it up on poles, over what had been the bungalow floor.

Mrs. Bobbsey, with the help of Bert and Nan, had managed to cook a meal over a camp-fire. There was very little wind, and the open fire would do no damage. So when Bill and Mr. Bobbsey returned a meal was ready for them. Bill wanted to go home, but the twins teased him so that he remained and ate with them.

Hardly was this simple meal out of the way when the van with the big tent arrived, and with it men who helped clear away the wreck of the bungalow and put up the canvas house.

"Oh, it's a big tent!" cried Bert, who, with Nan, had ridden a little way with Bill on his way home, and who had walked back in time to see the tent being unloaded.

"I'm glad, in a way, that the bungalow blew down," said Nan to her older brother. "It's lots more fun to camp in a tent."

"I think so, too," he agreed.

Flossie and Freddie were fairly squealing with delight as they raced about, getting in the way of the men, but no one minded this.

By late afternoon the tent had been erected over the old bungalow floor, the logs of the former shack were piled up with Mr. Bobbsey's timber, and what food could be saved from the wreck, together with that brought from the farmhouse, was put in boxes that formed a pantry in the tent.

The tent was divided off by hanging curtains of canvas so there were separate rooms. In sunny weather they could eat at a table outside, and when it rained they could dine inside the tent.

Before dark, with the help of the children, the new camp was fixed up so that the Bobbseys could spend the night in comfort. Blankets and bedclothes had been saved from the wreck of the bungalow and dried and these were put on the beds that Mr. Bobbsey had had sent up with the tent.

A hurried supper was eaten, and then a fire was built in front of the tent to make the place more cheerful, not that it was really cold, though the nights were cooler than the days.

"Did you hear anything more about the lumbermen who may have taken the things from our bungalow?" asked Mrs. Bobbsey of her husband, in a low voice, as they sat before the camp-fire.

"No," he answered. "And I made some inquiries in town when I went after the tent. It's a good thing we had Bill's wagon, for I could bring more in that than in the car. No, I didn't hear anything about the men, but someone certainly took our things."

"It's strange they haven't bothered any more about your timber," said his wife.

"They'd better not!" exclaimed Mr. Bobbsey, with a laugh. "Those men will get into trouble with me if they try to take my logs."

Bert piled more wood on the fire, and he was just going to propose a game that he and the other twins might play when suddenly the quiet of the forest was broken by a strange cry. It was a terrifying scream that broke out in the night—a cry like that of a child in pain.

"Oh, my! What's that?" exclaimed Mrs. Bobbsey, while Freddie and Flossie ran to their father's side, and even Nan dropped the stick she had been about to throw on the fire and moved towards her mother.

CHAPTER XIII

SHINY EYES IS GONE

MR. BOBBSEY, who had arisen from his place by the fire to look around the tent and see that all was secure for the night, paused as he heard that terrifying cry and glanced up at the dark trees on which flickered the blaze from the camp-fire.

Again came the strange moaning cry, like some child in pain.

"Oh, what is it?" asked Mrs. Bobbsey. "Someone is being hurt, Dick! Maybe a child is in trouble of some sort."

"Listen!" whispered Mr. Bobbsey.

There was silence for a moment, then Flossie sobbed out:

"I—I don't want to stay here! I want to go back to my own home, I do!"

"Hush! Hush!" soothed her mother. "Keep quiet."

There was a rustle in one of the trees, and Mr. Bobbsey saw something moving amid the branches.

"Get out of there! Scat!" cried the father of the

Bobbsey twins. At the same time he threw a chunk of wood up into the tree. Then he threw a stone.

Again came that strange cry, and mingled with it was another that caused the Bobbsey twins to exclaim in surprise. Then a body of some animal scrambled down the tree and ran off in the darkness.

"What made you say 'scat', Daddy?" asked Freddie, in curiosity. "That's what you say to a cat."

"Yes, and it was a *cat* I was saying it to," answered Mr. Bobbsey, with a laugh. He looked much relieved.

"Oh, was that a *cat* making that terrible noise?" asked Nan.

"A sort of cat," her father answered. "But not the kind of pussy we have at home. That was a bobcat, or lynx."

"Are they dangerous?" asked Mrs. Bobbsey. "I should think any animal that made such a horrible sound would be dangerous," she added.

"The bobcat, or lynx, isn't dangerous if you leave it alone," said Mr. Bobbsey. "It will never come after you or attack you, though it might take chickens or ducks if it got the chance.

"I suppose this bobcat saw our fire and wanted to know who had come to live in his woods," he went on, with a laugh. "But don't be afraid—he'll never bother us again. I think he has gone to some other part of the forest by now."

"What makes 'em call him bobcat?" Freddie questioned, with wide-open eyes. "Is his name Bob?"

"No, it is called that because it has a short, or

bobbed, tail," replied his father, with a laugh. "And now don't worry any more about it. The cat came here to have a look at us, it climbed up in a tree and sang us its little song and now has gone away."

"Well, if you call that singing," laughed Mrs. Bobbsey, "I never want to hear any more."

"No, I should say not!" agreed Nan. "It sounded like a baby. Indeed it did to me, Mother."

"Yes, a bobcat does cry in rather a human way," agreed Mr. Bobbsey. "And sometimes hunters have been fooled by it. I didn't know we had any in these woods. But, after all, they are not dangerous. That is, if you let them alone. They will fight if cornered."

The Bobbsey twins felt sure their father knew what he was talking about, for he had been in the woods year after year and was quite a hunter himself, as well as a lumberman. So Flossie and Freddie and Bert and Nan gave no further thought to the bobcat. Except that Bert, as he went to bed later in the evening, said to Nan:

"I wish I could catch a bobcat. Wouldn't it be great?"

"Maybe after you got him you'd wish you didn't have him," observed Nan.

"Oh, I'm not afraid," boasted Bert. But I think he was glad his father and mother were sleeping in the same tent with him.

Mrs. Bobbsey for some time lay awake listening to the noises of the forest all about them and to the lapping of the water on the shore of the lake. But they were not disturbed by any more wild howls and the night passed quietly.

"Well, we are really camping out now," said Mr. Bobbsey, the next morning, when breakfast was being cooked on the oil stove, for one of these very useful articles had come with the tent.

"Camp-fires are very pretty to look at and jolly to read about, but when you are in a hurry for breakfast there is nothing like an oil stove," Mrs. Bobbsey said. "And certainly, on rainy days it is much more comfortable cooking in the tent over an oil stove than standing near a smoking camp-fire that will not burn."

"Yes, we are really camping out now," agreed Bert, as he brought a pail of water from the lake so the smaller twins could wash. "It's lots more fun than the bungalow. Don't you think so?"

"The bungalow was nice while it lasted," observed Nan.

"But it didn't last long in that storm," laughed her mother. "Yes, I think the tent is very nice, and it is healthy for sleeping in at night—plenty of fresh air."

There was still much to be done about the camp to put it in proper shape for the two or more weeks the Bobbseys would live in it. The night before only so much had been done as was really needful. Now with a full day ahead of them, the campers began putting things "shipshape", as Mr. Bobbsey called it—that is, making everything neat and tidy.

Bert and Nan helped their father and mother at this, and as Freddie and Flossie could not be expected to do much, the smaller twins were allowed to play about as they pleased.

"I'm going fishing!" declared Freddie, and he got the rod and line his father had given to him for his last birthday. It was a real hook on a real line, and Freddie knew how to be careful so he would not catch the sharp barbs in his fingers, nor stick Flossie with them. And, more than once, from the little dock to which the boats were moored, Freddie had caught small sunfish and perch.

"I'll get Miss Shiny Eyes," announced Flossie. Shiny Eyes was the name of her best-loved rag doll—a doll who had two shiny, metal buttons for eyes. That is how she got her name—"Shiny Eyes".

"All right," agreed Freddie. "You get Miss Shiny Eyes and I'll catch some fish for her to eat."

So while Bert and Nan helped their father and mother, Flossie and Freddie had fun on the dock.

"You don't need to stay here much longer, Dick," said Mrs. Bobbsey to her husband. "I know you want to see about getting men to move your logs before some of those bad characters take them away. We can get along here very well now. You go after your helpers."

"I should like to go and see if everything is all right," admitted Mr. Bobbsey. "So if you think you can manage here——"

"Oh, of course we can," replied his wife. "Run along, Daddy! With my four twins I'll manage even the bobcat!" and she laughed merrily.

"The bobcat won't even so much as howl during

the daytime," said Mr. Bobbsey, as he went into the tent to get his hat and coat. "Be good children, now," he called to Flossie and Freddie and Bert and Nan, as he rowed away, for he was going by boat across the lake to make further arrangements about shipping his logs.

"Do you mind if I go fishing, Mother?" asked Bert, when he had finished several chores around the tent, little tasks that his mother asked him to do. Nan was busy making a cake which would be baked in the oven that went on top of the oil stove.

"No, Bert, I don't mind," his mother answered. "Go fishing if you like, and if you catch some large ones—not like the baby fish Freddie catches—I'll fry them for your Daddy's supper."

"I'll catch you a whale!" promised Bert.

"Don't!" begged Nan, with a laugh. "We haven't any pan large enough to fry it in. Don't catch a whale."

"All right," agreed Bert, and then he went off with rod and line to find a good spot along the shore of the lake for fishing. Freddie begged to be taken along, but Bert shook his head, saying:

"You stay here, Freddie. You'll be the only man in camp after I go, and mother needs a man in camp; don't you, Mother?" Bert asked, with a glance to show that he wanted Freddie to remain behind.

"I'd like to have Freddie stay with me," answered Mrs. Bobbsey, and you may be sure after this that nothing could have induced Freddie to go away. He wanted to protect his mother.

The two smaller children played on the dock, Freddie now and then catching a fish, which caused great excitement—at least, as far as he and Flossie were concerned. Nan finished her cake, and it turned out a beautiful brown. Mrs. Bobbsey had made up the beds and was thinking it was nearly time to get lunch when Flossie, who had been up in the tent to get a clean dress for her doll, came running back up the slope from the lake crying:

"She's gone! She's gone!"

"Who?" asked Nan, gazing at her little sister in surprise.

"My doll!" wailed Flossie. "Shiny Eyes is gone! Somebody has taken my doll!"

CHAPTER XIV

ROAST CORN

FLOSSIE felt so bad about her lost doll and her tears were so real that Nan took pity on the little sister and went down to the dock with her. Nan could remember the time, not so long ago, when she, too, would have cried had anything happened to one of her dolls. Now, though Nan still liked dolls, she did not play with them as much as she used to.

"Maybe Shiny Eyes fell into the water," suggested Nan.

"Oh, no, she couldn't!" insisted Flossie. "I left her right in the middle of the dock, and she couldn't get in the water except she jumped up and walked, and Shiny Eyes couldn't do that."

"No," agreed Nan, "a rag doll can't walk. Well, I'll look and maybe I can find her for you."

"Is anything the matter?" called Mrs. Bobbsey from the tent, as she saw Nan and Flossie hurrying to the dock, on the end of which Freddie was fishing. "Has anything happened?"

"Flossie has lost Shiny Eyes," explained Nan. "That's all."

"No, I didn't lost her," cried Flossie. "She lost herself." The golden-haired twin was so worried and upset that she got her words all muddled up.

Mrs. Bobbsey went back into the tent to finish making up the beds ready for the night, and Flossie and Nan continued on their way to the dock.

"Now show me where you left your doll," said Nan to her little sister.

"Right here, where I was having a play party for her," answered the blue-eyed twin. "I made a little table and I went up to the tent to get a clean dress for Miss Shiny Eyes and when I came back she wasn't here. I looked all around, too."

Nan could see where Flossie had started to fix up a little table for the doll, with shells for dishes and bits of leaves and shiny pebbles for things to eat. But the rag doll, with the two gleaming buttons for eyes, was not to be seen.

On the end of the dock Freddie was tossing in his baited hook and pulling it out again, almost before a fish had time to nibble. Suddenly Nan had an idea.

"Maybe Freddie caught his fish hook in your doll's dress and pulled her into the water," suggested Nan. "I guess that's how it happened that your doll can't be found."

"No, I didn't do that!" declared Freddie, when Nan asked him about it. "I couldn't do that—my fishline doesn't reach back that far."

This was true. Standing on the end of the dock,

where he had been all the while Flossie was playing with her doll, Freddie could not toss his hook far enough back to catch in the doll's dress.

There was no doubt about it, Shiny Eyes was gone, and Freddie had had nothing to do with her going. As Flossie had said, the doll could not get up by herself and walk off the dock. Someone or something must have taken her.

"But who or what was it that would do such a thing?" asked Nan.

"I don't know," half sobbed Flossie. "But Shiny Eyes is gone!"

Nor could Nan imagine what had happened. If this had taken place at home or at Meadow Brook, Nan would have guessed that some other boy or girl had come up slyly, and, just for fun, had hidden Flossie's doll. But here there were no other children —at least not near enough to make it possible for them to have taken the doll.

True, there was Bill Stoddard, but he lived over a mile away, and Bill was too old a boy to play with dolls or to take them to tease a little girl.

"Never mind, Flossie," said Nan, after a time, during which she had looked all over the dock for the doll but had not found it. "Never mind. You can play with another doll, and maybe some time Shiny Eyes will come back to you."

"Maybe she will," agreed Flossie, who was easily amused. "I'll go get my rubber doll, and if she falls into the water it won't hurt her."

While Flossie was getting out her rubber doll Nan

was talking to her mother about the strange disappearance of Shiny Eyes. Mrs. Bobbsey listened with interest.

"Someone must have taken the doll off the dock, Mother!" insisted Nan. "Do you suppose it could have been that bobcat we heard last night?"

"I don't think so," answered Mrs. Bobbsey. "You heard Daddy say those animals never come around in the daytime, especially where people are."

"Well, then maybe it was one of the bad men who wanted to take Daddy's logs," went on Nan. "They might have taken Flossie's doll, Mother."

"Oh, nonsense!" laughed Mrs. Bobbsey. "A rough lumberman wouldn't want a rag doll, even if she had shiny buttons for eyes. What could a lumberman possibly want of a doll, Nan?"

"He might want it for his little girl—if he had one."

"Oh, no, I hardly think so," remarked Mrs. Bobbsey. "I think that Flossie, without knowing it, or perhaps Freddie, knocked the doll into the lake."

"But it would be floating near the dock then," declared Nan. "It was a rag doll and wouldn't sink."

"Well, I'm sure I don't know what has become of it," said Mrs. Bobbsey. "Only don't imagine the bobcat or a lumberman took Shiny Eyes."

And so the lost doll became one of the mysteries of the Bobbsey camp—a mystery that was not solved until a few days later. Meanwhile Flossie almost forgot about Shiny Eyes and was content to play with some of her other dolls, a number of which had been brought along to Lake Melrose in the car.

Daddy Bobbsey returned in time for lunch, and Bert was lucky enough to land two good-sized fish which were fried until they were crisp and brown.

"I guess we'd better live up here all the year," chuckled Mr. Bobbsey, as he ate the fish Bert had caught. "It's cheaper than living at home. Our meals wouldn't cost us much if Bert had luck like this every day."

"I guess maybe I couldn't catch many when the lake froze over," admitted Bert. "But it's fun up here now."

"I caught a fish, too," said Freddie.

"But it jiggled off the hook," added Flossie. She had seen this happen, so she knew.

"Anyway, I caught him," insisted Freddie.

Mr. Bobbsey was told about the missing doll, but he did not think much about it, for he had other matters on his mind—such as getting his logs afloat and keeping the bad men from taking them. He thought, as Mrs. Bobbsey did, that one of the smaller twins must have knocked Shiny Eyes off the pier into the lake, where she perhaps caught on a part of the pier under water and was held there.

"Well, we are camping out now in great shape," said Mr. Bobbsey, as he looked around the neat tent. "Aren't you glad you didn't give up and go home after the bungalow blew down?" he asked his wife.

"Yes, I am," she admitted. "But how is your business coming on? Are the men to be here soon to roll the logs into the lake and float them down to your mill?"

"Yes, in a day or so," was his answer. "They are busy on another piece of work now, so we shall have to wait a while. But we shall enjoy ourselves meanwhile." And enjoy life the Bobbseys did.

There was little to do while waiting for Mr. Bobbsey's lumbermen to come for the logs, and during the long days, towards the end of summer, Daddy and Mother, with the twins, often went about the lake or in the woods on picnics and excursions.

Sometimes they would walk, and at other times they would go in the boat or the car. They paid visits, now and then, to the farm of the Stoddard family, and had more than one jolly meal there. Bill, though older than Bert, often came to the tent to visit and play games.

One day Mr. Stoddard came in from the field, just as the Bobbsey family was about to go back to camp after a visit. Mr. Stoddard had his arms filled with ears of green corn.

"Take some of these along," offered the farmer to Mr. Bobbsey. "They are fine roasting ears and if you build a camp-fire out in front of your tent you can have a feast tonight or tomorrow."

"Thanks, I'll do it!" said Mr. Bobbsey. "I haven't been to a corn roast for a good long while."

"Say, is it pop corn?" Freddie wanted to know.

"Pop corn will come later, little man," answered Mr. Stoddard, as he placed some of the roasting ears in the Bobbseys' car. "But you will like these almost as well. Just wait and see."

And that night there was a corn roast in front of the big white tent in the woods on the shore of Lake Melrose. Mr. Bobbsey knew just how to heat some stones on the edge of the fire, and to get the embers red hot so they would roast the juicy kernels without smoking or burning them.

Then, when the corn was roasted, the Bobbseys sat about on logs for seats, and while the camp-fire gleamed they ate the delicious food.

"Have some more, Freddie?" asked his father, when he saw the little fellow lay aside one gnawed ear.

"No—no, thank you, Daddy," was the answer. "I—I'm—full!"

"How about you, Flossie?" asked Mr. Bobbsey.

"Oh, don't tease them to have any more," laughed Mrs. Bobbsey. "They have eaten so much now that I'm afraid they'll be ill in the night. They've had enough, Dick."

"Perhaps they have," he admitted. "But we have a lot of corn left," and he glanced at a pile of raw ears. "We'll boil that for dinner tomorrow."

But the next day something happened.

The raw ears of green corn had been placed in a pile at the corner of the tent outside, to keep them fresh. Towards noon Mrs. Bobbsey sent Nan to get the corn, intending to boil it for dinner, as Mr. Bobbsey had suggested.

But Nan came running back to her mother, her eyes big with excitement.

"Where's the corn?" asked Mrs. Bobbsey.

"I didn't—it's gone—some of it—and there—there's an animal with hands taking more!" burst out Nan.

"An animal with hands!" cried Mrs. Bobbsey.

"Yes, an animal with little black hands is taking the green corn!" went on Nan. "Oh, Mother! Come and see!"

CHAPTER XV

THE BRUSH FIRE

MRS. BOBBSEY hardly believed what Nan had said—about an animal with "hands". She thought possibly Nan had seen a big rat taking away an ear of corn, and, in a way, the forepaws of a rat do look a little like hands.

"What's the matter?" asked Bert, when he saw his mother and his twin sister hurrying around the corner of the tent.

"Nan says some animal is taking the corn," answered Mrs. Bobbsey.

"Whoop!" yelled Bert. "Me for that animal!" He caught up a club.

"Don't be rash," his mother advised him.

"What sort of an animal is it, Nan?" Bert asked.

"It's got hands," declared his sister.

"Is it big?" Bert questioned.

"Oh, not so very, but it looked at me fierce!" asserted Nan.

"Whoop!" yelled Bert again. "I'm going to——"

"Be quiet. You'll scare it away," ordered Nan.

"Well, isn't that what you want to do—to keep it from taking the corn?" asked Bert, who had started for the corn pile.

"I want Mother to see what kind of animal it is first," said Nan.

The three of them turned the corner of the tent and there, standing near the pile of corn and greedily eating the tender, juicy kernels, was an animal with a long pointed nose. A band of black fur ran across the eyes and under the chin. The greyish fur was thick and heavy, and the tail was ringed with bands of whiter fur.

As Nan, her mother and her brother looked, the animal picked up an ear of corn with its front paws which, as Nan had said, were almost exactly like small, black hands, and, holding the ear thus, the animal stripped off the husk and began eating the kernels.

"There!" excitedly whispered Nan. "What did I tell you? See the hands!"

"Whoop!" yelled Bert, and at the sound of his voice the animal dropped the corn and scuttled away in fright.

"He's easily scared!" laughed Bert.

"What was it, Mother? What was it—the animal with hands that ate our corn?" asked Nan.

"That was a raccoon," answered Mrs. Bobbsey. "I have seen them before, and I should have remembered when you spoke of 'hands', Nan. No other animal, except perhaps the monkey, has anything so nearly like our hands. In the way the raccoon can use his front claws and paws they are certainly like hands. And there is another queer thing about raccoons."

"Do you mean the rings on his tail?" asked Bert. "He's like the Old Lady from Banbury Cross, only she had rings on her fingers and bells on her toes."

"No, I don't mean the rings on the tail of the raccoon," went on Mrs. Bobbsey, "though they are odd enough. But you have seen the raccoon eating the only kind of food he will take without washing it."

"Washing his food, Mother!" cried Bert. "Does he do that?"

"Yes," answered Mrs. Bobbsey. "That is one other queer thing about raccoons—they are very clean animals. No raccoon will, if he can help it, eat meat, fish or plant roots without first washing every bit that he eats. Perhaps in winter, when everything is frozen, he may not be able to wash his food. But when he can, he does—even raccoons that are kept in zoological parks.

"However, he never bothers to wash green corn. I suppose he is so fond of it that he thinks if he stopped to wash it some other animal might get it away from him. Anyhow, green corn is the only food a raccoon doesn't wash."

"Maybe on account of the husk on corn, the raccoon knows it's clean enough to eat without washing," suggested Nan.

"Maybe," agreed her mother.

"It's like a banana, corn is," said Bert. "It keeps

clean inside the husk just as a banana keeps clean inside its skin."

"Perhaps that may be the reason the raccoon doesn't wash the corn," agreed Mother Bobbsey. "Well, you have seen a strange and interesting sight, and, even if the raccoon did take some of the ears, we have enough left for lunch."

Only a few of the green ears had been gnawed by the raccoon before Nan saw him, and these could easily be spared. While lunch was being prepared, Bert set off by himself to trace the raccoon home to its den. The boy wanted to see the little animal at work washing some of its food.

And he was rewarded. Going softly through the forest, Bert came upon a hollow tree where some raccoons lived. He was lucky enough to see the two older raccoons getting a meal in a pond. And in the mud on the edge of the pond Bert saw some marks that looked like those a baby's foot would have left. These were made by the hind paws of the raccoons, which make a mark almost exactly like a baby's bare foot, for raccoons, like men and bears, walk with their heels on the ground, not like dogs and horses and cows, upon their toes.

Hiding behind a bush and keeping very quiet, Bert saw one of the raccoons wade into the shallow pond and begin feeling around in the mud of the bottom. Soon the mother raccoon caught a frog, which she killed, and then, dipping it in the water several times, she washed it clean before she ate it. The other raccoon did the same thing.

Then Bert saw the raccoons dig up some roots of a plant growing near the edge of the pond. And before these roots were eaten the queer animals, with rings of dark-coloured fur on their tails, washed the roots, which formed a sort of dessert to their meal of frogs.

Bert was not satisfied with watching the raccoons from behind the bush. He wanted to see their nest close at hand, so he went up to the hollow tree. Then the raccoons saw him and ran away, but Bert kept on to the nest.

The boy thought he might see some baby raccoons, but it was too late in the season for them, the little raccoons were now well grown. They were not at home, having, very likely, gone off hunting for themselves.

But, on looking around the hollow tree, in which the raccoons had made their home, a hole high up in the trunk forming the door, Bert saw something that made him open his eyes in wonder. And this something was a rag doll with shiny buttons for eyes lying in a huddled heap on a pile of leaves at the foot of the tree.

"Flossie's doll!" cried Bert. "Flossie's doll, Shiny Eyes! How did it get here?"

He picked up the doll, which was little the worse from its stay in the woods, and looked it all over. On one arm was the mark of a muddy paw, just the kind of paw a raccoon had.

"One of the raccoons must have sneaked out on the dock and picked up Shiny Eyes!" cried Bert. "That's why Flossie couldn't find her doll! The raccoon took it! But I'll take it back to my sister!"

When Bert brought the doll back to the tent, telling where he had found Shiny Eyes, and when he told about seeing the raccoons washing their food, Mr. Bobbsey said:

"There is no doubt about it, the raccoon took Flossie's doll. Raccoons are very curious, and anything bright and shiny attracts them. That's how hunters catch them in traps. Instead of baiting the trap with something good to eat, they will put on it a shiny bit of tin. The raccoon sees this glisten in the sun and he just can't keep from coming closer to see what it is. Then he wants to take hold of it, and when he tries to pick it up the trap is sprung and he is caught. Poor raccoon!"

"Then he must have seen the sun shining on the metal buttons that are the eyes of Flossie's doll," said Mrs. Bobbsey.

"That's exactly it!" said Mr. Bobbsey. "And the raccoon wanted the doll because the eyes were shiny. You must be careful, after this, Flossie, to cover your doll with a blanket if you leave her on the dock."

"I'm never going to leave her there any more!" cried Flossie, hugging her doll closely. "I don't want those 'coons to take her."

"They didn't harm her," said Nan. "Do you think they took her inside the tree, Bert?"

"I couldn't tell. I found her on the ground outside. Maybe a little girl raccoon took your doll home, Flossie," went on Bert, "and when she got it to the hollow tree maybe her brothers wouldn't have a doll in the nest, so they threw it out on the leaves."

"They shouldn't have thrown out my doll!" cried Flossie. "She's a good doll and I love her," and she held Shiny Eyes closer.

So that is how Flossie's doll was taken away and brought back. Rather strange, you may say, but if you know anything about raccoons you will agree that even stranger things than this have happened.

The Bobbseys talked for many days about the odd event, and once, led by Bert, the other children had a glimpse of raccoons on the shore of the pond, near their tree, washing their food.

As the days passed, Mr. Bobbsey cleaned up the litter of leaves and broken wood caused by the blowing down of the bungalow, and to this stuff he added bits of brush until he had quite a pile on the shore of the lake.

"I think I'll burn that brush," he said to his wife one morning. "It will be in the way when the men come to roll the logs to the lake, so I may as well burn it and get rid of it."

"Won't it be dangerous?" asked Mrs. Bobbsey.

"I think not," her husband answered. "There is no wind now, and the brush will soon burn."

"It will make a big camp-fire!" cried Bert, when told what his father was going to do.

Making sure that the smaller twins were well out of the way, Mr. Bobbsey lighted the great pile of brush and refuse from the ruins of the blown-down bungalow. Up leaped a pillar of smoke gleaming here and there with bright flames.

"Hurray!" cried Bert, who had been allowed to light one side of the pile.

Everything seemed to be going well for a time, and the fire was not endangering anything near it.

"The place will be neat and clean when we get all that trash burned," said Mr. Bobbsey.

But suddenly the wind, of which there had been not a trace at first, began to blow. It ruffled the waters of Lake Melrose and then began driving sparks towards the woods, and towards that part of the woods on the edge of which Mr. Bobbsey's logs were piled.

"Dick!" cried Mrs. Bobbsey, running into the tent after her husband, who, having started the fire, had gone to look at some papers about his lumber business. "Dick! Come quick! The fire is spreading!"

As Mr. Bobbsey rushed out he saw sparks from the brush pile start a blaze in the bushes near his timber. Fanned by the rising wind, the brush fire was spreading.

"This will never do!" cried Mr. Bobbsey. "There's danger here!"

CHAPTER XVI

TO THE RESCUE

MR. BOBBSEY'S cries of alarm caused more fright to the twins, and they were already frightened enough by seeing the fire spread. Though, at the same time, they rather enjoyed the excitement.

"Nan," Mrs. Bobbsey called to her older girl, "you take Flossie and Freddie down to the lake and out in the boat, but don't go too far from shore."

"Do you want us to get water to splash on the fire?" asked Flossie, as she watched the growing blaze.

"If we had a hose it would be lots of fun to squirt on the fire, the way we sprinkled Dinah," added Freddie.

"You can't do anything like that now," said Mrs. Bobbsey firmly, as she watched her husband catch up a pail and run to the lake to fill it with water. "Take them out in the boat, Nan, but don't go too far from shore. They'll be safe from any flying sparks when on the water."

Then Nan knew the reason her mother wanted her

to take charge of the smaller twins; it was so they would be out of danger when Mr. Bobbsey fought the fire, as he was now getting ready to do.

"I'll help!" exclaimed Bert, as he took another pail and ran after his father towards the lake.

"Yes, and I must help too," said Mrs. Bobbsey, as she found a pail. "If this fire isn't checked soon, the whole woods may catch, and the timber will burn."

"Our tent might blaze up, too, mightn't it?" asked Bert.

"Well, I hope not. The wind isn't blowing that way now, though it may change any minute," his father answered. "But that's a lesser thing. The woods mustn't catch! Work fast now, Bert, and don't talk—save your breath for carrying water."

The three Bobbseys ran back and forth between the lake and the edge of the brush fire, which was slowly eating its way into the woods. On one trip Mr. and Mrs. Bobbsey and Bert carried full pails of water, which they splashed on the blaze, causing loud hisses and clouds of steam to arise. On the other trips they carried the empty pails to the edge of the lake, and on these journeys they could go faster as they had no heavy weight of water to burden them.

Nan got into the boat with Flossie and Freddie and pushed out from shore a little way. It was all she could do to keep the smaller twins in the boat, as they wanted to get out and go back to help fight the fire that was spreading rapidly.

Freddie had often said he wanted to be a fireman,

and he thought this was as good a chance as he would ever get to practice.

"I can throw on water!" he cried. "I could squirt water, if I had a hose! Why won't somebody get me a hose?"

"Yes, I guess you could—you've done it before," said Nan, with a laugh.

Back and forth, back and forth ran Mr. and Mrs. Bobbsey and Bert, with empty pails and full pails. But all the water they splashed on the blaze did not seem to be doing very much good.

"It's getting away from us, I'm afraid," said Mr. Bobbsey, pausing for a moment's rest after dashing on a pail of water. "It's getting worse every minute."

"What are we going to do?" his wife anxiously asked.

Mr. Bobbsey was about to say that he did not know what could be done, as there was no fire department at that part of the lake. The wind, too, shifted and blew sparks towards the tent. Just as the campers were becoming very much frightened there was a sudden shout, and through the forest came running several men and boys.

"We'll help! We'll help!" they yelled. "We'll help!"

Bert had time to notice that one of the men was Mr. Stoddard, the farmer, and his son Bill was among the boys.

"We saw this smoke," explained Mr. Stoddard, as he ran to the lake to fill a pail he had brought with him. "We guessed that you'd started a fire and that you'd let it get away from you."

"That's about what happened," admitted Mr. Bobbsey. "I didn't know fire would spread so, but I ought to have known better than to take any chances."

"Well, 'tisn't too late yet—we'll soon douse this!" cried Mr. Stoddard. "Get busy, friends!" he added.

The fire-fighters—farmers and their boys who had come to the rescue when they saw the clouds of black smoke—lost no time in dashing water on the blaze as Mr. Bobbsey, his wife and Bert had been doing.

And now, with more hands to carry the pails, there was a better chance of putting out the blazing brush. Back and forth they rushed. Bert was, as he said later, having "the time of his life", and Nan said afterwards she wished she could have helped. But she was needed to look after Flossie and Freddie in the boat, where they were kept out of danger. It was no easy matter to quieten Freddie, who kept insisting:

"I'm going to be a fireman when I grow up, and I want to help put that fire out. I want to—to practice."

"But it's almost out now, Freddie," said Nan, and this was true. The rescuers had arrived just in time, and with their help Mr. and Mrs. Bobbsey and Bert were able to get the better of the blaze. The wind, which had threatened to carry big sparks into the woods, died away and this helped to stop the spread of the flames.

"There!" exclaimed Mr. Stoddard as he threw on a final pail of water, "I guess we've got the best of it. I'm mighty glad it was no worse."

"So am I," said Mr. Bobbsey, while Bert and the farm boys sat down to rest, for they were very tired. "I'll never start another brush fire so near the woods again," said the father of the twins.

"'Tisn't very safe," agreed another farmer. "Especially when the woods are so dry. Wet weather is the time to burn up brush, as it isn't so likely to spread."

"I ought to have remembered that," admitted Mr. Bobbsey. "I am a thousand times obliged to you folks for coming to help us. We were just about to give up."

"I thought you might have a peck or two of trouble on your hands when I saw smoke over this way, towards your camp," said Mr. Stoddard, as he wiped his face, which was streaked with black smoke and soot. "So I called Bill, and we rounded up some of the men and ran over here. Well, all's well that ends well, they say."

"And I'm glad of it," added Mrs. Bobbsey. "Now if you men and boys will sit down I'll make you some cool lemonade."

"That sounds good," replied Mr. Stoddard. "We are hot enough for it, goodness knows."

Nan, seeing the danger was over, brought to shore the boat with Flossie and Freddie in it, and then Nan helped her mother make the lemonade for the warm and weary fire-fighters.

"If it was winter they could have hot coffee," said Freddie, as he saw the lemonade glasses being passed around. "That's what they always give the firemen in winter. I know, 'cause I saw 'em have some once when our house was on fire."

"Our house wasn't on fire, Freddie," corrected Nan. "It was another house down the street."

"Well, anyhow, our house was *almost* on fire," said the little boy. "And the engines were in front of our house and I saw the firemen drink hot coffee 'cause it was cold."

"That part's right," admitted Bert with a laugh.

The last of the dangerous sparks had been doused with water, but to make sure there would be no starting up of the blaze in the night, Mr. Stoddard and the men and farmer boys walked through the woods around the piles of logs, looking for stray and glowing embers. They found none, however.

"Well, neighbour, you've had pretty hard luck since you came here to camp, haven't you?" said one farmer to Mr. Bobbsey.

"I should say he had!" exclaimed Mr. Stoddard. "First his bungalow blows down and then he nearly burns up his tent."

"And that isn't all," remarked Mr. Bobbsey. "While the bungalow was in ruins—before we could get back to it after the night we were lost—a lot of our things were stolen."

"Stolen!" cried Mr. Stoddard. "Do you mean taken away?"

"Just that," answered Mr. Bobbsey.

"What things?" asked one of the farm boys.

"Some of my papers, some clothing, a lot of food and other supplies," said Mr. Bobbsey. "At first we had an idea that thieves came while we were away, took what they wanted, and then wrecked the bungalow to cover it up. But afterwards I thought they may have come to the bungalow after the wind blew it down, and, thinking no one wanted the stuff, they may have helped themselves.

"I suppose it was a band of tramps, or men like that, who were wandering around the country. That's why I didn't think it was of any use to tell the police, though I would like to get back some of the things. But I suppose the tramps are very far from here now."

"It wasn't tramps who took your things!" exclaimed a boy named Henry Armstrong.

They all turned and looked at him.

"What makes you say that, Henry?" asked Mr. Stoddard.

"Because it was some lumbermen who took the things from the blown-down bungalow," the lad went on.

"How do you know?" asked Bill.

"Lumbermen!" exclaimed Mr. Bobbsey, and he looked at his wife in a strange manner.

"Yes, it was lumbermen," went on Henry. "And here's how I happen to know, though until now I didn't know it was this blown-down bungalow they were talking about.

"I was out in the woods the other day," related Henry, "and I got lost. I was in the deep part of the forest and I came to a little valley. I was going down in it, for I thought it would take me home, when I heard talking.

"As I didn't know just who it was I laid low—I hid, you understand," he said. "Then when the talk went on I crept a little closer. I saw an old log cabin, and the men were in there, talking. They were lumbermen, as I could tell by their talk, and they were laughing. One of 'em said:

"'Well this is pretty good fodder to get from the old bungalow!' And another one said: 'Yes, and we got a lot more than food!' Then somebody told 'em to keep quiet, and somebody else said maybe they'd be heard talking, and they grew quiet.

"But I heard enough to make certain that they were lumbermen and that they had taken things from an old bungalow. I didn't know it was this one here," and he nodded towards the place where the tent covered the foundation of the former house. "But now I know it must have been. So those were the men, Mr. Bobbsey, who must have taken your things."

"Yes, it does seem so," admitted the father of the Bobbsey twins.

"Are you sure they were lumbermen?" asked Mrs. Bobbsey.

"I'm certain of it," answered Henry Armstrong. "For they were talking of logs and of trees they had cut, and they said something about a man having cheated them of wages."

"That settles it!" cried Mr. Bobbsey. "They must have been the same lumbermen who were trying to stop me from taking my own logs."

"Did anything like that happen?" asked Mr. Stoddard.

"Pretty nearly," replied Mr. Bobbsey. "Of course I don't owe these men money, though they think I do, and maybe for that reason they came and took some of my things when the bungalow blew down."

"Well, we can't have things like that happening around here," declared Mr. Stoddard. "I'm a deputy constable—that's a sort of policeman," he explained to the twins. "And I'm going to see about these men. Do you know where to find them again, Henry?"

"Oh, yes, I could locate the place," was the lad's answer. "I found a short cut home after I heard the men talking, and I could easily find the place again."

"Then let's go after 'em!" cried Mr. Stoddard.

He was about to hurry away with some of the men, when Bill, looking through the woods to a point farther down the shore of the lake, called:

"Here come some men now!"

"Yes, and they're lumbermen!" cried Bert. "Look at their tools!"

A bunch of rough-looking men were approaching, and each one carried some implement of the lumber trade, a crowbar, an axe or the peculiar hook used for turning logs over.

"Oh!" exclaimed Mrs. Bobbsey in a low voice to her husband. "Maybe these are the bad lumbermen coming to take your logs!"

CHAPTER XVII

THE LUMBER RAFT

CERTAINLY the lumbermen who were stalking on towards the Bobbsey camp looked to be rough fellows, who would not stop at a fight to gain what they wanted. There were half a dozen of them—about the same number of men and boys as had come to fight the fire.

What could Mr. Bobbsey do to save his logs if these men wanted to take them in claim for money they thought was owed them? It did not seem that anything could be done. But Mr. Bobbsey was not the one to give up easily. Bert and Nan knew that, even if Flossie and Freddie, being younger, did not.

"Are these the men, Henry, you heard talking in the shack about having taken things from a ruined bungalow?" asked Mr. Stoddard, in a low voice.

The farmer boy shook his head as he answered:

"I couldn't be certain. I didn't get a good look at 'em."

On came the lumbermen, led by a tall chap who

seemed to be the foreman. Mr. Bobbsey looked about on those whom he might count as his friends—the men and boys who had come to help fight the fire.

"Mr. Stoddard," said Mr. Bobbsey, in a low voice, "there may be trouble, and I don't want you to get into it."

"What sort of trouble?" asked the farmer.

"When I came here to look after these logs I bought from a man around here, some lumbermen said they had a claim for wages," said Mr. Bobbsey. "These may be the same men, and they may try to take my logs."

"We won't let 'em!" exclaimed Mr. Stoddard.

"I'd rather you wouldn't get into trouble on my account," went on Mr. Bobbsey. "So if you want to leave now, and let me fight it out alone——"

"No, I wouldn't think of that!" cried Mr. Stoddard. "You're a neighbour of mine, and neighbours must stick together. We'll see what these fellows want."

By this time the leader of the approaching lumbermen was within talking distance. He stopped, looked curiously at the group of fire-fighters who had finished their lemonade, and then this man said:

"I'm looking for a Mr. Bobbsey."

"That's my name," answered the father of the twins.

"Glad to meet you. My name's Todd, Sam Todd," went on the other. "Mr. Sneed sent word to me that you wanted a gang of men to float some logs down to your mill on Lake Metoka."

A sigh of relief came from Mr. Bobbsey.

"I'm glad you have come," he said. "It's all right," he added to Mr. Stoddard and the others. "These are the men I hired to look after my timber. They aren't the ones who claimed I owed them."

"I'm glad of that," said Mr. Stoddard. "Now there won't be any trouble."

"No," answered Mr. Bobbsey. "It will be all right, and as soon as I can get the lumber rafted down the lake we'll close up our camp here. Funny—these were my own men and I didn't know it. But then I'd never seen them. I just told another man to hire them for me."

"Mr. Sneed couldn't come himself," went on Sam Todd, the foreman of Mr. Bobbsey's lumbermen. "But I guess we can look after matters for you."

"Yes, I guess so," agreed Mr. Bobbsey, with a smile.

"What you been trying to do here?" asked Sam, as he motioned to his men to lay off their coats and begin work. "Trying to burn the place down?"

"It does look that way," admitted Mr. Bobbsey, with a smile. "And before that the wind tried to blow us away. But we're all right now, thanks to these kind neighbours," and he nodded towards Mr. Stoddard and the others.

The situation was explained to Sam Todd, and Mr. Bobbsey told him how he wanted the logs made into rafts and floated down. Then the wind storm and the fire were mentioned, and the story was also told of the bad lumbermen who had taken things from the bungalow.

"Those fellows ought to be rounded up!" declared Sam Todd.

"We're going to get right after 'em," replied Mr. Stoddard. "I'm a deputy constable and I'll swear in some more men, neighbours of mine, to help me arrest these chaps."

"I hope they get the money that's coming to them," said Mr. Bobbsey. "Though certainly I don't owe it to them."

"It's queer they should say you do," remarked Sam Todd. "Who did you buy this lumber off?" he asked.

"A man named Kling, and I'm sure he wouldn't sell it to me if any of the choppers had a claim on it," Mr. Bobbsey answered.

"Well, no matter what sort of a claim they have on these logs," exclaimed Sam Todd with a laugh, "they won't have it long. My men will soon put these logs in the lake and you can cut 'em up into boards as soon as you're of a mind to."

"That's what I want to do," said Mr. Bobbsey. "And as soon as you start making up the rafts, Mr. Todd, I'll go with Mr. Stoddard and see if we can't round up these bad lumbermen."

"Can I come with you?" asked Bert, who, with the other twins, had been eagerly listening to all this talk.

"Oh, no, Bert!" said his mother.

"Why not? I'm big enough!" Bert said.

"And if there's another fire I'm going to help put it out!" cried Freddie, who felt rather out of things because he had not been allowed to carry water for the brush blaze.

"Well, we'll see about that," his mother told him.

Mr. Bobbsey talked a little longer with Mr. Stoddard, again thanking him and the other farmers for their services.

"And whenever you're ready we'll get after those tramp lumbermen in the shack," concluded Mr. Bobbsey. "I want the things they took from the 'busted bungalow', as Henry says they called it."

"That's what they did," asserted the farm boy who had overheard the talk.

"Well, I'll look for you in a day or so," said Mr. Stoddard, as he and his neighbours went back to their homes. "You'll be busy with your own lumbermen for a while."

"Yes, I expect I shall," admitted Mr. Bobbsey.

Then began a busy time at the camp of the Bobbsey twins. The lumbermen under Sam Todd first made a camp for themselves a little farther down the lake than where the tent stood. They built what they called a "lean-to", being a sort of three-sided shack made of poles.

"It's so warm nights we don't need much shelter," said Sam.

"But what are they going to eat?" asked Freddie. He meant to speak in a whisper, but he spoke louder than he intended.

"We eat pork and beans, mostly," said Sam Todd, with a laugh. "We do our own cooking, little man, so don't worry, thinking we'll take your grub."

"Oh, you could have some of ours! We have a lot!" offered Flossie.

"I'm afraid it wouldn't last long with my gang," chuckled Sam. "But we have our own cook and we'll get our own grub, Mr. Bobbsey. You just show me the logs you want rafted down and we'll do the rest."

"There are the logs," and Mr. Bobbsey pointed to the stacked timbers he had bought.

"We'll soon have them floating down the lake," promised Sam.

Then began a busy time in the camp—busier than ever before, except when the fire was burning. Having seen that Sam Todd and his men knew their business well and had started to rafting the logs, Mr. Bobbsey, a day or so later, said he thought he would go over and arrange with Mr. Stoddard about catching the thieving lumbermen.

"You'll be back before night, won't you?" his wife asked.

"Oh, yes," he answered. "It won't take long to catch those fellows, I think."

Nan, with Flossie, went off a little way from the camp to look for mushrooms, for Nan had learned to tell the poisonous ones from those that can be eaten. Mrs. Bobbsey was busy in the tent, setting things to rights. Bert and Freddie watched the lumbermen for a while, and then Freddie said:

"I know where we can make a raft of our own, Bert."

"Where?" asked Bert.

"Over in that little cove," went on Freddie, pointing to one near the larger cove where the men were fastening logs into big rafts. "There's a lot of little logs over there," said Freddie. "The men don't want 'em. I asked Mr. Todd and he said they didn't. We can take 'em and make 'em into a raft."

"Say, that'll be fun!" cried Bert. "We'll go on a voyage!"

The two boys found the smaller logs, odds and ends the lumbermen said were not worth putting in the big rafts, and Bert and Freddie were soon making a raft of their own.

And on it they were to have strange adventures, and not a little danger.

CHAPTER XVIII

WAS IT A BEAR?

ALL that morning Freddie and Bert worked on their raft. They had seen how the lumbermen fastened the big logs together with slender saplings, nailed fast from one floating tree trunk to another.

"We could use wild grape vines," suggested Bert, when he and his small brother found that nailing the saplings was hard work.

"Let's take a lunch along and go on a voyage—like Robinson Crusoe," proposed Freddie, always eager for adventure.

"All right!" agreed Bert.

When their log raft was made, they found it would easily support them in the water. They tried it in the cove while the raft was tied fast to a stump on shore, with a wild grape vine for a rope.

"We'll build a cabin on our raft, and then we can take Flossie and Nan," suggested Freddie.

"It will take too long to make a cabin now," Bert said.

But Freddie brought some empty boxes down to the shore and they were put on the raft for seats.

"Well, they'll keep our feet dry," Bert admitted, as he helped his small brother put the boxes on the raft. "Because when we get out in the lake the waves will wash up on us if we don't sit on the boxes."

"It will be fun!" cried Freddie. "I'll get a lot of things to eat."

The boys had lunch in the tent with their mother and sisters. Mr. Bobbsey had not yet returned, being off with the farmers trying to find the tramp lumbermen. The other lumbermen, who were building Mr. Bobbsey's rafts, had their dinner in their own camp.

"What are you going to do with all those things?" asked Mrs. Bobbsey, as she saw Freddie piling bread, meat and cake into one of the baskets which had been taken on the picnic—the picnic when the campers had to remain out all night. "What are you going to do with all that food, Freddie?"

"Oh, Bert and I are going on a voyage—like Robinson Crusoe," Freddie answered.

"It's all right," Bert told his mother, with a laugh. "Freddie and I have made a raft and we're going to sail on it. We just thought we'd take a little grub along in case we got shipwrecked," and he grinned at his mother.

"Oh!" exclaimed Mrs. Bobbsey. "That's all right," she added.

Now she understood. Bert was letting Freddie have the fun of taking the food along, though Bert did not believe half of it would be eaten.

Even though they went voyaging down the lake shore a mile or so they would be back before night, Bert thought, so there was really no need for food. But it pleased Freddie to pack up a lunch, and Bert did not mind humouring his small brother.

"Be careful," cautioned Mrs. Bobbsey, as the two boys started for the cove where their raft was moored, carrying with them a basket of provisions. "Don't go out too far and don't stay too late. Daddy will expect to see you at supper time."

"We'll be back," promised Bert.

"And maybe we'll catch a bear!" added Freddie.

"Pooh! If you see a bear you'll run!" laughed Flossie.

"I will not!" Freddie declared.

For a wonder Flossie did not tease to be taken with her brothers on their raft. But she and Nan had found a pleasant place to play in the woods behind the log pile, and Flossie was anxious to go back there with Nan after dinner.

So the two boys were allowed to do as they pleased with the raft they had made. Mrs. Bobbsey was not anxious, for she knew each of them could swim, and she trusted Bert to look after his small brother.

While the lumbermen were getting ready to set afloat one of the big rafts of Mr. Bobbsey's logs, the two boys loosed their small one from the mooring stump and poled out into the lake.

"It's just like a real voyage!" cried Freddie, in

delight, as he looked at the boxes on the raft, and one of the boxes contained the basket of food.

"Yes, it's fun," agreed Bert. "If we had a sail now it would be a lot more fun."

"Let's make one," proposed Freddie eagerly.

"No, not now, we haven't time," objected Bert. "Let's go along the way we are. We can make a sail tomorrow."

This satisfied Freddie and he helped Bert push the raft by means of long poles away from the shore. As the two boys on their queer craft moved out beyond the point of the cove, some of Sam Todd's workers saw them.

"Look at those kids!" exclaimed one lumberman. "They're trying to learn our trade, I reckon."

"They've made a pretty good little raft," observed another. "It'll stand quite a wind without breaking up."

"Well, we're going to have a breeze soon, if I'm any guesser," remarked Sam Todd. "I hope those kids don't go out too far. If they do, we may have to row after them and bring them back."

Waving their hands to the lumbermen, Bert and Freddie poled their raft out into the lake till the wind began to carry it along. There was not much of a current in the lake, not enough to have moved the raft at a faster pace than that of a mud turtle. But the wind did what the current did not do—it sent the raft along at a good rate of speed.

"We're travelling fast, Freddie!" cried Bert, as he saw objects on shore seeming to slip past them.

"Yes, it's almost as good as a sail," Freddie agreed.

Indeed the bodies of the boys, as they stood up on the raft, acted somewhat like a sail. And the boxes, too, served to catch the wind as the breeze gained in force.

The wind was now rippling the lake, sending little waves over the tops of the logs.

"Oh, my feets is getting wet!" cried Freddie, forgetting, in his excitement, to talk properly.

"Sit up on a box," replied Bert, as he did so himself. "It's a good thing you brought the boxes along, Freddie."

"And I brought the food, too," added the little fellow. "Shall we eat now?"

"Oh, no!" laughed Bert. "We just had dinner. Save it until we're hungry."

"I'm hungry now—a little bit," returned Freddie.

"You're always that way, so a little won't hurt," chuckled Bert. "We'll wait a while."

Along the shore of the lake, blown by the wind, went the boys' raft. They passed the white camping tent, and Mrs. Bobbsey waved to them, as the lumbermen had. Then Freddie and Bert turned another point of land and the camp was lost to sight.

Bert had rigged up what might be called a rudder for the raft, though all it was, really, was a broken oar fastened to the rear, or stern, of the bunch of logs. But it served to steer the raft towards or away from shore.

"We're getting out a bit too far," said Bert, after a while. "I guess we'd better go in a bit, Freddie."

Freddie was willing to leave it all to Bert, happy enough to be thus voyaging and adventuring with his older brother. So Bert headed in towards shore.

"There's a little island!" cried Freddie, pointing to one just ahead. "Let's land there and eat."

"All right," agreed Bert, with a laugh. "You won't be happy until you dig into the food, I suppose."

The island was a small one—not much larger than the raft itself—and was not far from shore. Bert and Freddie had no trouble in landing on it, and, having made their raft fast, they went ashore, "like Robinson Crusoe," Freddie said.

"Yes, it is a little like that, except that we aren't shipwrecked yet," agreed Bert.

"Maybe we shall be!" said Freddie hopefully. "Anyhow, if we are we have lots to eat," and he took with him the basket of food.

"You brought along enough for three or four meals!" laughed Bert, when he saw how much his small brother had packed into the basket. But afterwards Bert was glad Freddie had done that very thing.

Sitting under a tree on the little island, the boys ate some of the food they had brought with them. The sun shone and sparkled on the rippling waters of Lake Melrose, and the wind caused the waves to lap the shore and the raft with a curious, slapping sound.

"Well, let's travel on some more," proposed Freddie, after they had eaten the "snack", as Bert called the lunch.

"We mustn't go too far," objected the older boy. But when they were afloat once more the motion of the raft was so pleasant and the wind blew it along so easily that Bert forgot about not going too far, and they travelled on and on.

"There's another island. Let's land on that!" proposed Freddie, pointing to a larger spot of land out from the shore of the lake.

"No, I think we've gone far enough," Bert said. "It's getting late and we'd better turn around and go back home. We have to be back at camp before dark."

Bert tried to steer the raft around by means of the oar he had fixed at the stern for a rudder. But a raft is not like a boat. It does not steer as easily. And though Bert succeeded in heading the raft towards the mainland, he could not turn it around. And, even if he had been able to turn it, he could not have sailed back against the wind. He had forgotten about that.

Even boats with all kinds of sails cannot sail directly against the wind. They have to tack, or zigzag, back and forth. But the raft could not do even that. It could only drift before the wind, and that is what it was doing now. It would not turn around and sail back towards camp, no matter how hard Bert pushed on the steering oar.

"What's the matter?" asked Freddie, as soon as he saw that his brother was having trouble. "Can't we get back?"

"It doesn't look so," Bert answered. "The wind is blowing harder. We can't sail against it."

"What are we going to do?" asked Freddie.

"Oh, we'll go ashore and walk back to camp," Bert answered. "Don't worry, we'll soon be on shore."

He gave up trying to turn the raft about. It was easy enough to guide it towards shore with the wind blowing as it was, though the shore was farther off, and it took longer to reach it than Bert had thought.

The sky that had been blue and smiling began to cloud over, and there were signs of a storm. The day grew darker towards sunset, and now that the end of August was near the days were not as long as they had been.

So it was nearly dark when the raft grounded on a shallow, sandy beach in a little cove. Freddie and Bert tied their craft to an overhanging tree on shore and then left the raft. All about them was woods, and the forest was growing darker every minute.

"Where are we?" Freddie cried.

"Oh, we're not far from home," Bert answered. "We'll just walk back and then we'll come here tomorrow and get our raft. Come on, Freddie."

"Wait a minute," called the little fellow, going back on the raft.

"What do you want?" asked Bert.

"I want to get our food," Freddie answered. "I'm —I'm getting hungry again."

"Yes, maybe it will be a good thing to take the food," agreed Bert. "Well, now let's see what sort of a walker you are."

As they were about to set off through the forest,

from which the last glow of the sunset had faded, they heard a noise in the bushes.

"Did you hear that?" asked Freddie.

"Yes," whispered Bert, "I did."

"Was it—was it a bear?" asked Freddie, in a hoarse voice.

CHAPTER XIX

AN ANXIOUS SEARCH

MRS. BOBBSEY came to the door of the tent and looked towards Nan and Flossie, who were playing not far away. Farther off in the woods could be heard the talk of the lumbermen and the rumble of big logs as they were rolled down from the pile to be made up into rafts and floated down the lake.

"Oh, Nan!" called Mrs. Bobbsey. "Do you see anything of Bert and Freddie?"

"No, Mother, I don't," Nan answered.

"They went off on a raft to see Robinson Crusoe," added Flossie.

"I know they went on a raft," said Mrs. Bobbsey. "But it is getting late now—almost time for supper—and they should be back. Don't you see them?"

From where they were playing Nan and Flossie had a better view of the lake than had Mrs. Bobbsey up in the tent. Nan now turned towards the water and looked carefully along the shore to see if she could catch a glimpse of her brothers poling back on the raft upon which they had started off some hours before. But all she could see in the lake were some distant boats sailing to and fro, and, nearer shore, Mr. Bobbsey's logs floating on the blue water.

"No, I don't see Bert and Freddie," called Nan to her mother.

"They shouldn't have gone so far away," said the mother of the twins. "I told them not to. But children are so thoughtless!" she added, with a sigh. She was beginning to feel that Bert was "growing up".

Having finished the "housework" in the tent and with everything ready for supper, Mrs. Bobbsey strolled down to the lake shore with the intention of looking along it herself, to make certain Bert and Freddie were not in sight.

They were not, as we know, being at that moment more than a mile from camp in a strange cove and with the wind blowing against them so that they could not sail back on their little raft.

Mrs. Bobbsey was no more successful than Nan had been in getting a sight of the missing ones, and as the shadows grew longer the twins' mother became worried.

"I wish those boys hadn't gone so far away," she murmured.

Nan and Flossie finished their play and joined their mother on the shore of the lake. Then all three gazed up and down the stretch of the water for a glimpse of the two boys. But the raft was not in sight.

"If Freddie's late for supper he sha'n't have any of the tarts, shall he, Mother?" asked Flossie.

Mrs. Bobbsey had made jam tarts that afternoon, and they were a special treat. Often, at home, she used to threaten if the boys were late for supper they would get no dessert, and Flossie was thinking of this threat now.

"Well, we'll see how late they are," said Mrs. Bobbsey. "It is almost supper time now. I wish your father would come. I wonder if he found the bad lumbermen and got back the things they took."

There was, as yet, no sight nor sound of Mr. Bobbsey. But he had said he would be back before dark, and his family knew he would keep his word.

The lumbermen, having done all they could that day, had stopped work, and had gone on to their own camp by a path through the woods behind the tent, so they did not, as yet, know that Bert and Freddie had not returned.

It grew darker rapidly, as it always does towards the end of August, particularly in the woods, and with the lengthening shadows the anxious look deepened on Mrs. Bobbsey's face.

"I don't see what's keeping them," she murmured.

"Maybe they went to meet Daddy," suggested Nan.

"They couldn't do that," Mrs. Bobbsey answered.

"Your father went over that way," and she pointed to the woods behind them in the direction of Mr. Stoddard's farm. "And Bert and Freddie went on their raft down that way," and she motioned to the right, down the shore of the lake.

"Let's go down that way and maybe we'll see them," proposed Nan, when it was evident that her brothers could not have gone to meet their father, who was on land while they were on water.

"Yes, we'll take a little walk along the shore," agreed Mrs. Bobbsey. "But we mustn't go too far, for your father might come back any moment, and if we weren't in sight he'd worry."

Down the path along the lake went Mrs. Bobbsey and the girls. Here and there the bushes grew so high that they could not see out across the water, but there were many places where the underbrush was low enough to glance over the top and here Mrs. Bobbsey gazed long and anxiously.

There was no sight of the raft and the two boys. Mrs. Bobbsey then noticed how hard the wind was blowing and the thought came to her mind that perhaps Bert and Freddie could not get back. This was, in fact, exactly the trouble.

"Maybe they're shipwrecked," suggested Flossie. "I heard Freddie say he wished they'd be shipwrecked like Robinson Crusoe. And he took lots to eat, so if they did get shipwrecked they needn't be hungry."

"Yes, I know they took plenty of food," said Mrs. Bobbsey, with a half smile. "But it would be hard to wreck a raft. I guess they went so far they can't get back, and they've started to walk. I only hope they don't get lost," she added, with another anxious sigh.

"Could they walk around and meet Daddy and Mr. Stoddard?" asked Nan, who wanted to help her mother.

"Oh, no. It would be too far and roundabout," was the answer. "They must be down this way, but it's getting too dark to go any farther. We must go back to the tent. Daddy may come at any moment."

As they walked back to camp they saw Mr. Bobbsey returning. The four of them met near the tent.

"Well, I had good luck!" exclaimed Mr. Bobbsey.

"Did you?" asked his wife, and for the moment he did not notice how anxious she was.

"Yes," answered Mr. Bobbsey. "We found the shack where the tramp lumbermen were stopping. We got back a lot of the things they took from our broken bungalow. They said they didn't think anyone wanted the stuff. But they might have known we did.

"They promised not to annoy me any more and they are going away from this part of the country. I guess we won't be bothered by them any longer."

"Did you have them arrested?" Nan wanted to know.

Mr. Bobbsey shook his head.

"No," he answered, "I didn't. I felt rather sorry for them. They are poor, and someone has cheated them of their wages. It seems they really did chop down these logs I now own, but they did it for another man, and they have a claim against him and not against me. So we have settled all our trouble, and Mr. Stoddard is keeping our stuff that we got back from the lumbermen until I can go after it tomorrow."

"Well, I'm glad your troubles are over," said Mrs. Bobbsey. "But there is more trouble here," she added, with a sigh.

"What do you mean?" asked Mr. Bobbsey. "Have the lumbermen who are making my rafts stopped work? Or have they taken some of my logs?"

"No, nothing like that," said Mrs. Bobbsey.

"It's Freddie and Bert!" burst out Flossie. "They went to see Robinson Crusoe and haven't come home!"

"How did they go?" asked Mr. Bobbsey quickly, with a look at his wife and a glance around camp.

"On a raft they made," she answered. "We have been looking for them, but can't find them."

"I guess they poled down too far and can't get back against the wind that is now blowing," went on Mr. Bobbsey. "They are, very likely, walking home through the woods."

"That's what I thought," said his wife. "But it's late and getting dark, and——"

"Come on," interrupted Mr. Bobbsey. "We'll start off and look for them. It only means a late supper, and I don't suppose they meant to get lost and give us trouble. We'll find them."

But this was easier said than done, and as the darkness settled down over the forest and the camp the search for the missing ones became more anxious. Mr. and Mrs. Bobbsey called and shouted the names of Freddie and Bert, but there were no answers.

CHAPTER XX

DOWN IN A HOLE

"SAY, Bert, it—it's getting awful dark, isn't it?" whispered Freddie, as, after they had stepped from their raft, he and his brother stood in the woods near the edge of the lake. "It's awful dark!"

"Oh, not so very," answered Bert, with what he tried to make a jolly laugh. "The moon will be up pretty soon, I guess."

"Do you think that was a bear we heard?" went on Freddie.

They had heard a noise in the bushes as they were about to set off to walk back to their camp, and Freddie's first thought was that the noise might have been caused by a bear.

"No, I don't believe it was," Bert answered. "A bear makes more noise than that, and I didn't hear any growls."

"No, I didn't either," said Freddie, hopefully. "And bears always growl. I like to hear bears' growls in a circus, but not here," he added. "Specially when it's so—so dark like!"

"It is getting dark," admitted Bert. "But then," he was quick to add, "I guess the moon will be up in a little while. Come on, Freddie, we must hurry to get back to camp for supper."

"We've something to eat here," Freddie said. "But of course we want to go home," he hastened to add.

"That's right, we have got some food left!" agreed Bert, with a laugh. "Let's eat as we go along. Then we'll not be so late getting home."

They had paused to listen to the noise in the bushes—a noise they had each feared might mean a bear—but now that this noise had stopped they set out again. They took some sandwiches from the basket of lunch they had put up and ate these as they walked along.

There was a path along the lake shore, a path that trailed in and out among the trees and bushes. At points where the path ran near the lake it was still quite light, in spite of the fact that the sun had set, and an evening glow was over the water. But when the boys had to strike in towards the forest, as the path wound that way, they walked in darkness, for the trees shut off what little light there was.

"Don't go so fast, Bert!" begged Freddie, after a while. "My legs is tired!"

"Oh, I forgot you didn't have such long legs as I have," Bert remarked. "We'll go a bit slower. Do you want me to carry you, Freddie? I can do it easy enough!"

"No!" answered the little fellow. "I can walk all right if you don't go too fast."

On they trudged, Bert now beside Freddie and holding his hand. Bert also carried the basket with what was left of the lunch. There was not much, for two hungry boys can eat a great deal in the course of an afternoon.

"How far do you s'pose it is back to camp?" asked Freddie, when they had walked on for perhaps five minutes.

"Oh, not far now," Bert answered. "We'll soon be there."

"But it's getting darker," went on Freddie. "You can't see."

"Yes, I can! I'm like a cat," said the older brother. "I can see in the dark."

In silence they trudged on, now and then stumbling over rocks or tree branches that littered the ground, for it was now quite dark. Suddenly Freddie grasped Bert's hand more tightly and whispered:

"There's one now!"

"One what?" Bert asked.

"One cat—what you said you were like. See those eyes!"

Freddie pointed up into a tree at the right of the path and amid the dark branches and leaves Bert caught sight of two gleaming green points of light reflecting the glow of some distant star or a last flicker of daylight from the sky overhead.

As the boys looked, Freddie almost ready to whimper in fear, Bert saw the greenish points of light move, and he heard the rustle of leaves and branches.

"Oh, maybe it's a wildcat and he's going to jump on us!" yelled Freddie.

But a moment later the silence of the forest was broken by a loud voice calling:

"Who! Who! Tu-who!"

Freddie would have dashed away, pulling Bert after him, but the older boy kept a tight grasp on his brother's hand and held him there. Then Bert laughed.

"Aren't you—aren't you scared?" demanded Freddie.

"No, of course not!" Bert chuckled. "That was only a hoot owl, and he's more frightened than we are. There he goes!"

As Bert spoke a shadow seemed to flit through the woods over the heads of the boys. It was the owl flying away, and his wings, covered thickly with feathers, seemed to make scarcely more noise than a shadow.

Owls fly very quietly, much more quietly than other birds, and it is needful for them to do so, as in this way they can get close to the rats or mice they want to catch in the night, without the animals hearing the wing-beats.

The owl flitted silently through the forest. Probably it had no idea that it had so greatly frightened a little boy. All the owl cared for was something to eat, and night was its time for hunting. During the day it slept in some hollow tree, to come out after dark, when its eyesight was keener than during the bright day. So Bert might better have said that he could see after dark like an *owl*, rather than like a cat, though cats have good eyesight for prowling around after dark.

"Come on, now," called Bert to Freddie. "We'll soon be home."

It was all he could think of to say to the little fellow, though in his own heart Bert began to wonder and worry about getting home, or rather, back to camp. Just where it was and how far away he did not know.

The boys reached an open place in the woods, to which the path had led them. It was a bit lighter here, for they could see the stars; but the moon, of which Bert had spoken hopefully, did not come out, and Bert really did not know whether it would or not.

But as the brothers crossed the open glade something like a black shadow passed over their heads, and Freddie shrank close to Bert and gripped his hand hard.

"There's the owl again!" cried Freddie. "But he didn't ask who we were. I guess he knows us now."

"That wasn't an owl," said Bert, as he watched the shadow flit away in the darkness. "That was a bat."

"Will he hurt us?" Freddie wanted to know.

"Not a bit of it!" answered Bert. "He's only after beetles and mosquitoes that fly after dark."

"How can he see?" asked Freddie. "And how can he see not to bump into us. He flew terribly close to me—right over my head."

"Oh, a bat can see better than an owl," Bert declared. "Daddy read to me about 'em in a book. Bats, even blind ones, can fly all around a room without bumping into anything or hitting anybody in the room, the book said."

"How do they do it?" Freddie wanted to know, and Bert was glad he could tell a little about the bats, as it took Freddie's mind off the fear of being lost in the woods at night.

"I don't know exactly how they do it," Bert answered. "The book said a bat has nerves, or something, in its wings and can tell by the feel of the air when near anything, and then it turns so it won't bump into it. They even took a bat and put wax over its eyes so it couldn't see, and then they let it fly in a room with wires criss-crossed in it, and the bat never hit one wire."

"Who did that?" Freddie demanded, with interest.

"Oh, somebody that wrote the book Daddy was reading to me," Bert answered. "I guess it was what our teacher in school calls a 'speriment."

"I wish I had some—some 'speriment gum!" sighed Freddie.

"Oh, you mean spearmint! That's different," laughed Bert. "Well, maybe Nan or Flossie will have some when we get back to camp."

"I wish we were there now," sighed Freddie.

And Bert wished the same, though he did not say so. He felt that he must keep up the courage of his little brother.

On and on they wearily trudged through the forest.

It was still very dark, though a little glow, coming from somewhere over the tops of the tree, seemed to show that the moon was coming up, and Bert hoped that this would happen.

They had crossed the glade, or open space, and were once more about to plunge into the forest when Freddie shouted and called out:

"Look at the dog!"

"Where?" asked Bert quickly.

"Right by that big tree!" and Freddie pointed.

Bert saw a small animal slinking along, an animal with such a dark coat of fur, or hair, that it looked almost like a patch of the woods moving. Then, as he caught sight of the animal's tail, he said:

"That isn't a dog, Freddie."

"What is it—a—a wolf?" faltered the little boy.

"No, it's a fox," answered Bert. "I can tell by its big brush of a tail."

"Like mother's dusting brush," added Freddie.

"Yes," agreed Bert.

The fox silently slunk out of sight, making scarcely a sound.

"What's the fox doing out so late at night?" Freddie asked.

"He's hunting for something to eat," answered Bert.

"Would he eat the bat and the owl?"

"I guess he would if he could catch them," Bert answered. "But an owl and a bat are both as smart as a fox and I guess he'd have hard work to get either one. All three of them hunt at night, though."

"Night is good for animals and some birds and bats," remarked Freddie with a sigh. "But it isn't so nice when you're lost in the woods—'specially at night."

"Oh, well, we'll soon be home," consoled Bert. "Come on, now, make believe we're soldiers and have to march to capture the enemy."

This pleased Freddie and gave him a new thought for the moment. He and Bert trudged on through the dark woods, hoping they were on the right path that would lead them back to camp.

Suddenly Freddie seemed to pull away from the grasp of his brother's hand.

"Here! What's the matter?" cried Bert. "What are you doing?"

"I—I guess I'm falling—into a hole!" screamed Freddie.

Bert felt him slipping away. The next instant Bert, too, began to slip and slide, and a moment later he and Freddie had fallen into a deep hole, somewhere in the dense woods.

CHAPTER XXI

A DREARY NIGHT

MR. AND MRS. BOBBSEY, with Nan and Flossie, having searched and called in the woods about the tent for some time and getting no answer from the lost boys, finally stopped to rest.

"Where do you suppose they can be?" asked Nan anxiously.

"Oh, they're somewhere, not far away," her father answered. "But they're probably too far away to hear us."

"I'm hungry!" suddenly announced Flossie. "I wish Dinah was here to get me something to eat!"

"Why, my dear, I'll get you something to eat!" said Mrs. Bobbsey. "We have been forgetting all about supper," she added to her husband. "You must be hungry too—and Nan."

"Yes, I think it would be a good idea to eat now," said Mr. Bobbsey. "By the time we finish the boys will likely be here—late."

"I don't care how late they come—I'll give them

something," said Mrs. Bobbsey, with a sigh. "Only I do wish they'd come!"

"Oh, they will," her husband said. "It isn't the first time they've been late or lost, and it isn't really dark yet."

It was not, for the search for Bert and Freddie had begun before those two adventurers had started to land from their raft.

"Supper will be good for all of us," decided Mr. Bobbsey. "And then, after supper, if the boys aren't back, I'll get Sam Todd and some of his men and we'll have a regular searching party."

"That will be the best way," agreed Mrs. Bobbsey.

It cannot be said that either Mr. or Mrs. Bobbsey ate with good appetites, but Nan and Flossie managed to put away fair suppers. Flossie was really not worried, for she was not old enough to think of any dangers. But Nan worried a little bit, especially when she saw the anxious looks on the faces of her father and mother.

"Tell us what happened when you went after the bad lumbermen," suggested Mrs. Bobbsey, thinking the telling of this might take Nan's mind away from worry. "Did you have any trouble?"

"Oh, no," answered Mr. Bobbsey. "When the lumbermen in the shack saw us coming they were a bit ugly at first. But Mr. Stoddard had several big, husky men with him and when the lumberjacks saw them they calmed down.

"I told them what we were after and when we looked in their shack we found almost everything that was missing from our bungalow. They had eaten some of the canned things, and they offered to pay for them, but I said not to mind.

"Because, you see," added Mr. Bobbsey, "the men hadn't been treated fairly, though it wasn't my fault, even though I own the logs they cut down and stacked around here."

"How did it happen?" asked Mrs. Bobbsey, and even as she asked she kept listening to hear if Freddie and Bert were coming along. But their footsteps were not heard.

"It was like this," explained Mr. Bobbsey. "A man who owned the woodland sold to another man the right to cut logs. This man hired the lumberjacks to cut and stack the timber. Then the man who had hired them went away and sold the logs to another man, and I bought them from this man. Of course I paid for them, but I had nothing to do with the man who hired the lumberjacks to cut the logs."

"What made the lumbermen think you owed them money?" asked Nan.

"It seems that the man who hired them, and who ran away without paying them, is named Bobley. It is so nearly like my name of Bobbsey that when the men heard my name they thought I was Mr. Bobley, and they acted in an ugly manner towards me. They thought I was the one who had cheated them, and that's why they thought they had a right to take things from the blown-down bungalow to make up for their wages.

"But it is all right now and we'll have no more

trouble. I'll bring back the things tomorrow. And now, as we've finished supper, we'll go out into the woods and bring home Freddie and Bert," he added.

But, again, this was easier said than done. Searching and calling again and again in the woods about the tent brought no answers from the missing ones. It was now dark; and Mr. Bobbsey lighted two lanterns, one for himself and one for his wife. Mrs. Bobbsey insisted on joining in the search. Though it was tiresome for Flossie to walk, she could not be left alone in the tent, and Nan did not want to stay there with her.

The four of them searched and called as best they might, but without finding or hearing Freddie and Bert. Then, when it had grown late, Mr. Bobbsey said:

"I'm going to get Sam Todd and his men. You go back to the tent with Nan and Flossie," he added to his wife. "Sam and I will soon find those boys."

"I hope so," murmured Mrs. Bobbsey, with a sigh. "I can't see where they are!"

"They're probably having a lot of fun, imagining they're camping out," replied Mr. Bobbsey, trying to laugh, though, to tell the truth, he did not feel much like laughing. "You say they took along plenty to eat?"

"Yes, a whole basketful. Freddie packed it!" answered his wife.

"Oh, then they'll be all right!" said Daddy Bobbsey. "Now you go back to the tent and rest, and I'll get up the searching party."

Sam Todd was surprised when, a little later, Mr. Bobbsey called at the lumbermen's camp and told about the missing boys.

"That's too bad!" exclaimed Sam. "We saw the little fellows poling off down the lake on the raft, but we supposed they'd come back long since."

"No, they haven't," Mr. Bobbsey said. "I don't suppose they are very far away, but they must be lost."

"Very likely. But we'll find them!" declared Sam Todd. "Tumble out, men," he called to his "gang". The men had finished their suppers and were sitting about camp.

Lanterns were lighted and the search begun.

It was kept up all night, and though the woods were crossed and crossed again by means of paths and trails, not a sight or sound of the missing boys was come upon.

Now and then Mr. Bobbsey would go back to the tent to see if his wife and daughters were all right. Flossie had fallen asleep, and so had Nan, but Mrs. Bobbsey, with wide-open eyes, waited for any good news.

"I'm sorry to say there isn't any," said her husband, on his third return trip to the tent. "We can't find them."

"What do you suppose has happened?" asked Mrs. Bobbsey, who was now in tears.

"Nothing serious, I'm sure," Mr. Bobbsey answered. "I think they landed from the raft and went ashore. They started to make their way back to camp, but took the wrong path and ended at some house. Probably now they're safe in bed with some farmer, and he may be on his way to tell us."

"But if that had happened the farmer, whoever he was, should have been here long ago," objected Mrs. Bobbsey.

"Maybe Bert didn't know very well how to describe where our camp is located and the farmer hasn't been able to find us. Or maybe it's so far away from here that he hasn't had time to get here. The raft may have gone farther down the lake than we think."

"Yes, perhaps so," sighed Mrs. Bobbsey. "Well, I hope you find them."

"Oh, we shall!" declared Mr. Bobbsey, as he went back to take up the search, half-comforted, himself, by what he had said.

All through the night the search went on. The moon had risen and it was not as dark as it had been, but even the moon-gleams did not show where the two Bobbsey twins were.

It was the grey dawn of morning when Mr. Bobbsey came back to the tent, tired and discouraged. Mrs. Bobbsey had fallen into a doze, but started up.

"Did you find them?" she asked.

"No," her husband answered. "But we surely will soon. Or they may come home themselves when the sun rises. They've probably been sleeping in a hollow tree all night. I'm going to get Mr. Stoddard and we'll go in the car to all the farms around here. The boys may be at one of them.

"I'll have Todd and his men keep on searching

the woods and I'll visit the farms. We'll find the boys soon enough now that daylight has come. And we'll soon be laughing about this. As for Bert and Freddie, they probably slept better in their hollow tree than I did."

But of course Bert and Freddie were not in the hollow tree. They were down in a hole, and it is time we found out what happened to them that night.

CHAPTER XXII

NAN'S SLIDE

IT was rather a deep hole Bert and Freddie had fallen into. Luckily there was a thick carpet of leaves on the bottom of the hole, so when the boys fell into it they were only shaken up a bit, hardly even bruised. And no bones were broken, for which they could be thankful.

For a time, though, they were rather stunned. It was like the time Bert played football with some of his chums and one of them ran into Bert, knocking him down. For a few seconds Bert lay on the ground with a queer rumbling feeling in his head, unable to get up.

It was this way with both Bert and Freddie after they had slid into the hole, and they lay in a heap, huddled up on the bottom amid the leaves.

Then Freddie roused up enough to ask in a shaking voice:

"What happened? Did the fox come after us, Bert?"

"No, and the bat, nor the owl, didn't get after us, either," answered Bert. "I guess we just fell into a deep hole, that's all."

"What sort of hole?" Freddie demanded. "Is it a bear's den?"

"Oh, no," laughed Bert, looking around as well as he could in the darkness. "This isn't a bear's den, you can tell by the smell."

Freddie sniffed and sniffed again.

"I can't smell anything but leaves," he said. "Wet leaves."

"That's what I meant," replied Bert. "If there was a bear here it would smell sort of wid-like."

"You mean a—a circus smell," put in Freddie.

"That's it!" exclaimed Bert. "We're down in a hole, all right, and a deep one, too," he added, for just then the moon shone over the tree tops and the boys saw that they were down in a hole about ten feet square, and deeper than they were tall. Indeed the top of the hole was well above Bert's head, and farther than that above Freddie's. The sides, too, were straight up and down, and not slanting, so it was not going to be easy to climb out without help.

The leaves in the bottom on which the boys had fallen as if on a cushion, were old and matted together, showing that the hole had been dug some time before. Bert felt sure of this as he looked about him in the light of the moon.

"Maybe if a bear didn't live here this hole was made by somebody for a trap," suggested Freddie.

"Maybe," agreed Bert. "It's different from the trap I made," and he had to laugh as he thought how he had been caught in the log trap he had tried to set up.

"Have we got to stay here all night?" asked Freddie, as he got up and walked around. "Have we, Bert?"

"Well, I don't know about that," answered Bert, as he followed his brother. "It doesn't look so easy to get out of without a ladder. But, if we do have to stay here it will be warm. The wind doesn't blow down in this hole, that's sure."

That was true, for being down in the hollow the cool night wind swept over the heads of the boys without chilling them. And they had felt rather cold up to the time of falling into the hole.

"We can eat, too," Freddie went on. "I have the basket of food."

"Good!" cried Bert. "I'm glad you hung on to it."

He had let Freddie carry the basket just before the accident happened, and Freddie had not let go, even when he felt himself toppling into the hole.

Bert made up his mind that if there was a way of getting out of the hole he was going to find it. But after several trials he discovered that he could not climb up the steep, straight sides. And, even if he had been able to do so, he would not have been able to get Freddie out.

"I guess we'll have to stay here all night, Freddie," said Bert, after walking all about the hole and finding it the same on all four sides.

"Well, I'm not afraid if you let me snuggle up close to you and go to sleep," Freddie said. "I'm hungry. I'm going to eat and then I'm going to sleep."

"That's a good idea," declared Bert. "We can crawl under the leaves and keep warm. I mean the dry ones."

Fortunately there had been no rain for some time and the leaves on the bottom of the hole were mostly dry. Into these the boys burrowed after eating the last of their food.

Freddie fell asleep first, as was natural. He was weary, but lying down he felt rested. He had been hungry, but now his little stomach was filled, and he was warm as he snuggled down in the leaves against Bert. So it was no wonder he fell asleep.

Bert took a little longer to doze off. For a time he thought of how his mother would worry because he and Freddie did not return. His father would worry too, and Nan and Flossie might cry, Bert thought.

"But we're safe here," reasoned the boy, " and we can't get back to camp tonight in all the darkness. The best thing is to stay here, and in the morning I can easily take Freddie back to the tent."

Then, as there was nothing else to do, Bert fell asleep. Though their bed was none of the best, the boys were so tired from their day's sail on the raft and their tramp through the woods that not once did they wake up in the night. They were so soundly asleep that they did not hear the searchers calling, and

Mr. Bobbsey and his men did not go very near the hole.

Not so calm and peaceful was the night back at the Bobbsey camp. There was worry and there was sorrow. But when morning came they all felt certain the boys would now be found.

"I'm pretty sure they aren't in the woods," said Mr. Bobbsey, when a hurried breakfast was being eaten. "I feel positive they spent the night at some farmhouse, and now we must find them and bring them back."

"I hope you will!" replied Mrs. Bobbsey. "But I simply can't stand it to wait here all day doing nothing."

"And yet it will be hard to take you around to the different farms," said Mr. Bobbsey. "We are going to hurry a great deal."

"Then I'll take the girls and wander through the woods," said Mrs. Bobbsey. "We may come across Freddie and Bert there. We can shout to them."

"I hardly think you will," her husband said. "They're farther off."

But for all that Mrs. Bobbsey set out, with Flossie and Nan freshened after a good night's sleep.

Soon three searching parties were started. One consisted of Mr. Bobbsey and Mr. Stoddard, who were going from farm to farm in the car. Another was made up of Sam Todd and his men, who were to tramp through the woods. Then there was Mrs. Bobbsey, with Nan and Flossie.

Almost before they knew it Mrs. Bobbsey and her daughters found themselves more than a mile from camp. They had gone on and on, first along this path and then along another, now and then stopping to call the names of the missing boys.

Nan and Flossie wandered a little distance away from their mother, down what seemed a pleasant path covered thickly with leaves. Nan saw what she thought was a pile of poles and brush that looked as if it might have been an over-night shelter of someone lost in the woods.

"Bert! Freddie!" Nan cried, thinking perhaps the boys were in the shelter. There was no answer. Nan took a few steps forward and suddenly felt her feet slipping from beneath her. The next moment she slid into a hole.

"Oh, Nan! Where you going?" cried Flossie, who had lingered behind. "Wait for me!"

Flossie ran forward before Nan could tell her to be careful and keep back, and an instant later Flossie slid into the same leaf-filled hole into which Nan had slipped. As soon as the two girls got over the stunned shock of their fall they gave cries of surprise.

There, lying almost at their feet, cuddled together in the leaves, were Bert and Freddie, just opening their eyes after a long night's sleep!

"Oh! Oh, Bert!" gasped Nan.

"Freddie! Freddie!" shouted Flossie.

Through the woods came the voice of Mrs. Bobbsey calling:

"Flossie! Nan! Where are you? Don't get lost! Where are you?"

"We're down in a hole!" answered Nan joyously. "And we've found Freddie and Bert! Oh, we've found the boys!"

Mrs. Bobbsey could hardly believe what she heard.

"Are they all right?" she called. "Tell me: are they all right?"

"Sure, we're all right!" answered Bert for himself.

The next moment his mother was at the edge of the hole. After one look she went in search of a long, slim tree branch. This she found and reached it down into the hole. Nan grasped it and Mrs. Bobbsey soon pulled her up to the surface. Bert then helped his mother get up Flossie and Freddie, and then Bert himself managed to scramble out as Nan had done, holding to the tree branch while his mother and Nan pulled on the other end. This was the only way to get out of the hole without ladders.

"What happened to you, boys?" asked Mrs. Bobbsey, after she had kissed them and hugged them.

"We got lost," Bert answered.

"Didn't you hear us calling you?"

"No," he said. "I guess we must have been asleep. But I didn't know we were so near camp." As a matter of fact the two rafters had wandered back to within nearly a mile of the tent, but the searchers had not found them and their calls had not been answered.

"Oh, but I'm glad you're found!" exclaimed Mrs. Bobbsey.

"And I'll be glad when we have breakfast," remarked Bert.

"All our food's gone," added Freddie.

The wanderers were soon back at the tent, contentedly eating. News of their return soon spread. The searching parties were called in, and Mr. Bobbsey was informed of the good news by telephone to one of the farmhouses where he had stopped to make inquiries.

"Well, this is a great day!" cried Daddy Bobbsey, as he danced around with Flossie on one shoulder and Freddie on the other. "But more care in your Robinson Crusoe play, boys! No more getting really lost!"

"No!" agreed Bert, with a laugh. "I guess we did go too far. But we'll help you with your rafts now."

"You can watch the men, at any rate," said Mr. Bobbsey. "We must work hard from now on, for we have lost time."

Though there was hard work in getting the logs into the lake and rafting them down to Mr. Bobbsey's mill, there was still time for fun, and the Bobbsey twins enjoyed to the utmost their stay in the woods. The children were even allowed to ride part of the way on one of the big rafts of logs, but Mr. and Mrs. Bobbsey went with them to see that they came to no harm.

And so all ended happily. The lost were found, the lumbermen who had threatened to make trouble went away after getting their money from the man who owed them, and after the last of his logs were floated away Mr. Bobbsey took his family from camp to their home in Lakeport on Lake Metoka.

"And now for winter fun!" cried Bert.

"Yes, and Christmas!" added Nan.

And here we shall take leave of the Bobbsey twins.

Read more of the Twins' adventures in
"THE BOBBSEY TWINS ON A HOUSEBOAT"